COLTER'S HELL

GREG STRANDBERG

Big Sky Words Press, Missoula

Copyright © 2015 by Greg Strandberg

First paperback printing, 2015

Printed in the United States of America

ISBN: 151719573X
ISBN-13: 978-1517195731

See images of the places in this book, the guns mentioned, maps showing Indian tribes, and more:

http://www.bigskywords.com/montana-blog/what-is-colters-hell

ALSO BY GREG STRANDBERG

CONTENTS

Part III – Tracking

Part IV – Vengeance

Fort Raymond

The Yellowstone

Snowy Range

Big Horn Mountains

The Shoshone

Absaroka Range

The Snake River

Absaroka Range

The Big Horn

The Wind River

Wind River Range

M. NIRES

INTRODUCTION
A SHOT

The sun was bright, the sky was big, and it didn't seem like they'd find a better place in all of God's Creation.

Captain Meriwether Lewis put the butt of his rifle down on the ground and his arm up. "This will do," he said, and the three men behind him came to a stop. Two of them let out sighs.

"Haven't even gone ten miles yet," George Drouillard scoffed at the two. He adjusted his yellow head-cloth, which was soaked with sweat.

"My feet say otherwise," Joseph Field said with a frown.

"They don't *say* anything, but they sure do stink up a storm," Joseph's older brother Reubin said, and both he and George broke out laughing.

"Alright, alright," Lewis said ahead of them, picking up his rifle once again, "let's get to making camp."

The men nodded and started doing just that, happy to get a break from the hot July sun overhead. They were still following the small creek that'd branched off from the Marias River, one they were calling Birch Creek on account of the trees growing up on its banks. The spot they were at now had the trees on just one side, the north, while the south was open grassland for a quarter of a mile before the ground rose up into a rocky ridge of hills a hundred feet high.

"Sure this is a good spot, Captain?" George said as they started to unfurl the tarps and break out the cooking supplies.

"Why wouldn't it be, George?" Lewis already had one of his journals out and didn't bother to look up.

"Just seems a bit open is all, sir," the half-Shawnee half-French-Canadian scout said. The Field brothers stopped their unpacking for a moment to look the captain's way. Sensing the tension in the air, Lewis looked up, looked around, and then shook his head.

"This will do," he said a moment later, his pen beginning to move across the journal's pages once again. George shrugged and started unpacking.

~~~

Wolf Calf came to an abrupt stop, his long black hair swishing about as he did so. He kept his hair unbound and flowing long, for he thought it made him look more savage.

The seven other young Blackfeet Indian braves behind him came to a stop as well. They were more boys than braves, really – Wolf Calf had just turned 13-years old, and though there were a few as old as him, none were older. They were armed as well, with sturdy bow and arrows. Wolf Calf even had a rifle, a good one too, or so Calf Looking thought. He was also 13-years old, and while he didn't have the courage or as powerful a father like Wolf Calf did, he was fast and smart and the boys looked up to him.

Calf Looking and the others were looking up to Wolf Calf now, for he'd begun creeping toward the edge of the ridge, the better to look over. The others held back, knowing that whatever their leader had seen below could just as easily spot them above if they moved forward. They also held back because of Wolf Calf's temper. One look at the swollen black eye of Sidehill Calf could tell you that, and that'd only come about because the 11-year old had suggested they go back that morning. Wolf Calf hadn't agreed to that, and now Sidehill Calf was sulking in the back of the band, wanting to go home more than ever.

Calf Looking knew they couldn't go back, not yet at least. He was with the Skunk Band of the Pikuni Tribe of the Piegan Blackfeet Nation, and coming back into camp with nothing to show for their three days of hunting would lower their worth in the eyes of the other bands. Calf Looking knew full well that Buffalo Child's Otter Band was waiting for such an opportunity to move up in the eyes of the tribe. Buffalo Child was one of the tribe's three Wise Ones, back at camp and no doubt scheming how he could become full chief. If he could use the young braves' poor showing to make Stone Bear's Skunk Band look bad, then he certainly would. Stone Bear was Wolf Calf's father, and also a Wise One, though one that didn't have as much ambition, or at least didn't let it show as much as Buffalo Child did.

Calf Looking sighed. He knew he shouldn't be out with an opposing band of braves, but his father forbade him to go out. Silver Heart was the third Wise One of the tribe and he treated Calf Looking too much like his older brother had been treated. Dog Hair *may* have been obedient, but he wasn't brave. Calf Looking was, and that's why he was with the Skunk Band, braves who craved adventure and didn't hide from it. Still, Calf Looking knew that his father didn't get to his high position by being a coward. Silver Heart was indeed a powerful Wise One, and one that could take over when Chief He Who Shouts finally died. Wolf Calf knew that, and it was probably why he'd been pushing them so hard over the past day. Wolf Calf's own father had been adamant that they go out for three days only. Today was that third day, and there was no way they could make it back to the tribe by morning...unless they had some horses.

Wolf Calf reached the edge of the ridge and peered down. Sure enough, there was a small band of fur trappers, four of them it looked like, and they had quite a few supplies. They had even more guns, four the young Piegan boy thought to himself, but that's not what he was really interested in. The true prize were the horses, twenty-one of them, all milling about in the grass a short distance from the men's camp. They had Nez Perce markings on them too, and must have been traded by the western tribe.

Wolf Calf shook his head. The Blackfeet had cowed the Nez Perce, and they'd done so with the same guns the whites were carrying now, long-barreled rifles that sent shots far. Those shots came sudden and unexpectedly from horseback. The horses below had their legs hobbled, and Wolf Calf smiled – it'd be easy to cut the small ropes put in place so the horses wouldn't move too far, and then all they'd have to do was ride on out of there, back to the village, *and* the admiration of the tribe. His father would be proud of him and Wolf Calf would gain much honor. That honor would be increased, the young brave knew, if he could bring the weapons back as well. Then his own father might have a chance at becoming chief, not just Looking Calf's, or worse, Little Mouse's. The thought made the young Blackfoot brave smile. Wolf Calf slowly began pushing himself backward, and after a minute he was back with the other seven boys.

"Horses," he said as soon as he reached them, "twenty-one horses and just four men, whites."

"Trappers?" Sidehill Calf asked, and Wolf Calf nodded.

"Looks like it, and it also looks like they're armed pretty good."

"So we'll rush in after dark and take off with the horses before they know what hit 'em," Sidehill Calf said with a laugh, clapping Looking Calf on the back beside him. Several of the other braves smiled and mumbled their enthusiasm as well, even if Sidehill Calf was likely putting on a show, the better to get them home faster.

Although he was happy to see some of the youngest of the braves' enthusiasm return, Wolf Calf shook his head. "They'll be watching, the sentries I mean. I doubt these men will sleep without posting someone to watch."

"Then what do you suggest?" Calf Looking asked.

"That we go down there and talk with them," Wolf Calf said. That was met with silence, as well as a lot of shuffling feet and downward looks. "Ah, c'mon – don't tell me you're afraid," Wolf Calf continued. "Those men have a lot of stuff down there – they *want* to trade. Let's go and see what they're doing, try to win their confidence, and see if we can bed down near them. When we know most are asleep and the sentry is dozing off, we'll make our move and take the horses." The 13-year old stared at the other boys, most younger than him. Only Calf Looking met his gaze, and Wolf Calf held it for several moments. Finally Calf Looking nodded, drawing the other boys' attention.

"Alright," he said, "but let's be careful – those trappers have enough guns for twelve men, and we don't want to get hurt."

Wolf Calf smiled. "Of course!"

After that they began to move down toward the creek.

~~~

"Captain," George said as quietly as he could, and then a little louder when he saw that Captain Lewis hadn't heard him. Lewis looked over, and then toward what George was nodding at. There were Indians coming, a small band of them.

"Men," Lewis said loud enough to get the attention of the Field brothers a short distance away. The two were organizing the packs to fit Lewis's latest samples, and they looked over and then quickly got up at the sight of the Indians. "Take it easy," Lewis said after a moment as he started forward, "let's see what they want." He began moving forward, said "George," and the scout was quickly at his side.

"Blackfeet...or maybe A'anninen," he said, "I'm not really sure. Sure are young though, I'd say 10-years to 13-years old for the lot of 'em."

"Old enough to fight," Lewis said quietly as they drew near.

Wolf Calf came to a stop about twenty feet from the two whites, one of whom looked like he had a bit of Indian blood in him. He raised his hand up. Though still kept his bow in his other hand, it didn't have an arrow nocked to it.

Across the distance, Lewis also put his hand up in greeting, and said "hello." Beside him George said a few Indian greetings in various tribal tongues, and after the fourth the young boy nodded and spoke up. He spoke for a few moments and then George nodded.

"They're Piegan Blackfeet," George said, "from around this area. They're young, and likely out on a small scouting or hunting trip for a day or two."

Lewis nodded, and then turned around and called out to the Field brothers. "Bring up some of the trade gifts." The two brothers nodded and were soon rushing up with one of the packs. They started to hand it to Lewis but he shook his head. "Find them three items for gifts," he said.

Within moments Joseph had a medal, a small American flag, and a handkerchief out.

"Those will do," Lewis said with a nod when Joseph looked to him, and the young man got up and walked the items over to the boys.

Wolf Calf took the items even though he didn't really want them. He wanted horses and guns, and maybe some whiskey for his father, but he knew the whites weren't likely to part with those. Still, he took the trinkets offered him and passed them back for the others to look at.

"We've been out for three days and need to return to our village tomorrow," Wolf Calf said once Joseph was back near his brother. "May we camp here for the night?"

George translated and Lewis nodded immediately. "Yes, by all means, yes! Tell them that we're eager to trade with them, just as we've been trading with their counterparts, the Nez Perce, Shoshone, and Kootenai."

"Sir, I'm not sure you want to say all that," George said, "the Blackfeet–"

"Oh, nonsense!" Lewis said with a laugh. "Tell them, will you."

George frowned, but did as he was asked. He'd known from the reactions upon hearing the tribal names from Lewis, however, that the news wouldn't be received well. And it wasn't. There were mutterings from the other braves and Wolf Calf had to turn around and silence them. When he turned back, it was with a business-like smile.

"We appreciate the hospitality and also the gifts," he said, "but what we'd really like to trade for are horses and maybe even a few of your guns." Behind him, Calf Looking couldn't believe what he was hearing. He never would have had the gall to ask the whites for those things, but then he supposed that's why Wolf Calf was the leader of the Skunk Band in all but name and he wasn't even much of a follower of his own band.

George translated the boy's words and Lewis looked on for several moments before answering. Finally he spoke. "We're just four men in a much larger party," he said, "and we don't have enough of either horses or guns to trade at this time. If you meet us closer to the Mandan Villages, however, we could probably come to an arrangement."

The Mandan Villages, Wolf Calf thought after George translated the words, *the dogs!* Instead of saying that he smiled and said what the whites wanted to hear. "We'll tell that good news to the elders and chiefs of our tribe."

"Wonderful!" Lewis said after George translated, and the two groups settled in to making camp for the night.

~~~

The last dying embers of the whites' campfire crackled and popped, and Wolf Calf knew it was time. For hours now there'd been silence from the three sleeping men while the sentry hadn't moved in a good hour. It was time, and Wolf Calf got up to tell the others.

It was clear from the conversations they'd had while gambling that the whites were trouble. The fact that they were trading with whatever tribes they came across showed that they knew nothing of the politics of the land. The Shoshone were weak, and always had been, so why would the whites want to give them guns? And the Kootenai? Wolf Calf had to suppress a laugh when he thought of *that* tribe handling a gun. Most likely the first brave would point the barrel at his head and pull the trigger. He smiled in spite of himself – maybe giving the Kootenai guns *wasn't* such a bad idea.

Within moments Wolf Calf had all the members of the band up and ready. All knew the plan, for they'd discussed it before bedding down. Even Calf Looking had been silenced, mainly because of how the gambling had gone. Everyone knew that you couldn't beat a Blackfoot at a game of dice, though it seemed the whites hadn't. And then to have the audacity to only pay out in beads and fishhooks and buttons? Wolf Calf still wondered how he'd been able to stay his dagger from biting into one of the whites' throats over that insult. Alas, the whites would pay, and they'd do that as they should have all along, with their horses. Wolf Calf meant to take those horses, but he wasn't greedy and would only take his fair share. The whites would still have five to get back to the Mandan dogs with, while his father would have sixteen more to his name. With that kind of collateral, there was no way anyone would be able to challenge him for the title of chief, once He Who Shouts finally did them all a favor and wandered off into the wilderness to die.

Wolf Calf looked over at the others. He'd given Looking Calf his gun, for he'd never been that good of a shot with it at night. They and two others would go for the majority of the horses while Sidehill Calf and the rest of the braves would go after the rifles, and cause a diversion with them if need be. Wolf Calf knew that if the whites heard a few gunshots go off in the night, they'd likely jump down into the nearest hole they could find, and that meant they wouldn't be going after the horses. The other braves would slowly slip away into the night, providing cover fire if need be until the last was finally gone. The whites wouldn't know what hit 'em.

~ ~ ~

Joseph Field was dreaming of St. Louis, and the brothels the city held. He was well-known in them, and loved. Few, after all, could match his deep pockets, pockets that bulged with the proceeds of his vast fur trading empire. As usual, the choicest women were falling all over themselves before he'd even gotten fully into the door. One, the most beautiful and voluptuous brunette that Joseph had ever seen, came up to him. She started to reach out for his rifle, not his gun. Joseph's eyes narrowed. *This isn't right...*

...Joseph awoke from his dream of St. Louis and the wonders it held, and at just the right moment – there beside him was a young Blackfoot Indian, his hand but inches from Joseph's rifle.

Joseph didn't think – he didn't have to. His right hand shot out to grab the rifle, just as the Indian boy's hand had reached it as well. Joseph pushed down, keeping the loaded rifle down on the ground while at the same time reaching over with his left hand to the large knife that was fastened there. With a quick flip of the thumb he had its latch undone and the blade up and out. One swift motion brought it over his body and toward the Indian's. Whether the Blackfoot saw the approaching knife or not, Joseph didn't know, but it was soon entering into the Indian's side.

Sidehill Calf had indeed seen the knife coming his way, but he'd been too slow to react. The blade bit into his side, deeply, and the young brave was suddenly feeling faint and like he might just blow over should a breeze start up. He tried to get up, but the white whose gun he'd been trying to steal did so first, and was quickly bounding away. Sidehill Calf tried to rise and do the same, but for some reason, his legs wouldn't listen. His eyes were growing heavy as well, and he figured if he just laid down for a few moments...everything would be alright. He did so, and the blackness took him.

~ ~ ~

George awoke from the blackness of sleep with a start – something wasn't right. It took but a moment for him to know what, too. He bounced up off his bedroll, for the horses were whinnying and stomping and that could only mean one thing – the Blackfeet were stealing them.

He bounded out of the tent and was happy to see Joseph and Reuben doing the same nearby. A moment later the captain appeared from his, his McCormick pistol in his hand. His arm shot out into the black night, and George looked over.

"There!" the Captain shouted, and George could see the faint forms of the boys in the moonlight. Sure enough, they were already riding off with some of the animals. He started off at a run, just as Captain Lewis did the same, the Field brothers too.

Lewis sped after two of the Indian boys that were astride some of their horses, and leading quite a few of the others behind them. "Stop!" he shouted, both in English and Mandan and even a few other tribal languages he'd picked up along the way. Nothing seemed to work.

Ahead of Lewis, Wolf Calf turned around. It was he and Calf Looking that'd gone to the horses, hoping the other braves would cause the diversion needed for them to get away. So far three of the whites seemed to have taken the bait, but the last one hadn't. Worse, the young Blackfoot saw, the man had a small gun in his hand and was waving it above his head. He motioned for Calf Looking to take a look. The other mounted Blackfoot looked back, and as he did so, he brought up his musket. It was an old thing, a relic of the tribe really, but it worked...sort of, and if you were lucky. It worked best at dissuading others from attacking or even thinking of attacking, and Calf

Looking was sure it'd do that now too.

Captain Lewis saw the young Indian turn about and look at him, then motion to the boy at his side. That Blackfoot was armed, and though it was one of the oldest and most decrepit British flintlock muskets he'd seen in some time, he wasn't going to take the chance to see if the thing still fired or not. As the young boy turned about, Lewis brought up his pistol, took aim, and fired.

BOOM!

"Ugh!" Calf Looking grunted, then slumped slightly on the back of his horse. Wolf Calf looked over and his eyes went wide – his companion was clasping his hand over his stomach, blood running through his fingers.

Calf Looking looked up at Wolf Calf, his eyes wide and full of shock. "Wolf Calf..." he said, then began to slump over.

Wolf Calf kicked his horse and was right there beside Calf Looking, pulling him over onto his own mount. He kicked and shooed the other horses away, for this round of horse thieving had suddenly gone terribly wrong. The animals broke off their run and started to stand still, blocking the route the whites were taking behind them, and allowing the young brave to ride off with his wounded companion seated behind him. Seeing what had occurred, the other members of the Skunk Band also fled off into the night.

Lewis chased them another dozen yards, then let off as it became clear the Indians were going to get away. He started back toward the horses, and George who was rounding them up.

"I shot one, George," Lewis said as soon as he reached the half-Shawnee scout, "I shot one right in the stomach."

George gave his captain a hard look, then nodded. "What else could you do?"

Lewis shook his head. "It's not what I wanted to do,

George, not what I wanted to do at all."

George nodded, was about to offer some words of consolation, when the Field brothers appeared.

"Got one," Joseph said as he approached, "got one in the stomach with my knife, just when his hands were inches from my gun."

"Did he get away?" Lewis said, hoping he had, like the one he'd shot had. Their diplomatic mission had just turned into a debacle, Lewis knew. By wounding at least one Indian, and now two, Lewis had virtually guaranteed that the already hostile Blackfoot wouldn't likely deal with Americans in the future, at least not peacefully. In the space of just one night, years of work had gone down the drain...or had it? When Joseph shook his head, however, signaling that the Indian he'd stabbed was indeed dead, Lewis knew that it had.

The men looked to their captain, waiting for word on what to do. They were in a tight spot, just the four of them, and out in the middle of Blackfeet lands. Sergeants Ordway and Gass were still out there, too, though miles and miles to the east. Because of this incident, however, they could be in danger, especially if the Blackfeet decided to go on the warpath. No, Lewis knew, the only thing left to them now was to get on their horses and ride the hell out of there.

He looked over at George and the Field brothers. "Gather the horses and get packed up – we're riding out of here and we're not stopping until we reach the others at the Marias River."

The men nodded, and set about gathering the horses and their things. Lewis wandered over to the dead Indian while they were doing so. He shook his head when he reached him. *Just a boy,* he thought, *just a boy with his whole life ahead of him.* A thought came to the captain, and he reached into his jacket. There was still a small medal there, a trade trinket, but one that he remembered the Indians had been interested in. Lewis took it out and bent down, placing it on the body. It was just a small gesture, but perhaps the other Blackfeet would take it for what it was, an apology.

Within ten minutes they were riding away.

~~~

Wolf Calf waited until the whites were well away before he rode back to the campsite. There he saw Sidehill Calf's body and he dismounted. He shook his head when he saw his friend, then narrowed his eyes. Was that...yes, it was...one of the shiny medals the whites had had. Wolf Calf bent down and picked it up, then frowned. The whites thought they could dishonor Sidehill Calf in death, putting their religious symbols on him. It was an insult, a high insult, just as though they'd scalped him.

Wolf Calf took the medal and flung it into the nearby river. Then he set to work. It was hard work for the 13-year old, but the young Blackfoot got the young brave's body up on the horse. It'd be a long walk back to the Skunk Band's encampment along the main river, but they'd walk it and get back in a day, maybe two. It all depended on how much Calf Looking could walk on his own. At least they still had one horse, and if nothing else, a travois could be fashioned for Sidehill Calf's body. Usually Wolf Calf wouldn't care too much about his dead, but in this case the rest of the tribe would need to see the body.

He made it back to the bottom of the ridge, where the others were gathered. As soon as he reached them, however, he knew that something was wrong.

"How is he?" Wolf Calf said right away, but his words were only met by shaken heads. A few more steps brought the brave close enough to see Calf Looking, the brave's eyes wide and unseeing and staring straight up to where the Sky People lived. He was with them now, Wolf Calf knew, with them and happy.

Some who wouldn't be happy were the whites, Wolf Calf vowed. He'd remember them, remember what they looked like, remember what they were wearing. The yellow head-cloth the half-Shawnee had been wearing stood out in his mind most of all.

PART I – INTO THE WILDERNESS

1. THE OUTFIT

John Colter stared out at the late-spring landscape and smiled. He was heading back upriver, into the wilderness...where he belonged. To think, just a couple weeks before he'd been heading to St. Louis, ready to join civilization. That was all behind him now and for at least one more season he'd be where few white men had gone before.

For Colter, it'd be the third such season in a row. The first had been at Fort Mandan on the Upper Missouri in 1804-5; next had been Fort Clatsop on the Pacific over the winter of 1805-6; and after that it'd been trudging through the snow for a time with Forest and Joe before he went out on his own. That'd been 1806-7 and now here it was, June 1807. That meant he'd be up at the three forks of the Missouri for the winter of 1807-8, unless Manuel got something else into his mind. Colter looked over at the Spaniard, who was nibbling on a quill pen while staring into an account book with those black, beady eyes, and he suspected that would probably be the case. *Will the winter of 1808-9 be any different?* Colter thought to himself, a full five years after Captain Lewis had first offered him the rank of private at $5 a month?

"That looks like a man that's thinking he's made a mistake," Colter heard a voice say from behind him. He didn't need to look over his shoulder to know it was George Drouillard, the half-Shawnee, half-French-Canadian scout that'd accompanied him for three years on the Lewis and Clark Expedition.

"Mistake? No," Colter said. "It's just..."

"Just that you're wondering what you could be missing, there in St. Louis."

"Or at the Bank of St. Louis on Merchant Street, where my 299.87^{1/2}$ from the expedition is."

"Ha!" George laughed. "You've got it calculated out and all, even with the interest, don't you?" He laughed again. "You wouldn't know what to do with that much money if you had it, John!"

Colter frowned. George was probably right – he hadn't used money since that last thing he'd bought in St. Louis in May 1803, a new comb. He wondered if that shop was still there. The way the men had made it sound over the past couple weeks, the city had grown so much he wouldn't recognize it. *In another year,* he promised himself, *in another year I'll see it again.*

George walked off after that, along the gunwale of the boat. There were three boats in all, two of the same length and one that was longer and wider and full of most of their goods. The first boat was more than fifty feet long and eight feet across. Behind it came the long keelboat, seventy-five feet long in fact, and eighteen feet wide. Behind it was the third boat, the same proportions as the first. The keel boats were long and wide and difficult to get up the river. The Missouri was flowing toward the Mississippi, which itself flowed toward the Gulf of Mexico down near New Orleans, and that meant the men had a hard time getting the boats upriver to the Upper Missouri where the best fur trapping was. They managed it, at quite the slow pace against the four mile an hour current, and did so in three main ways.

First was cordelling, which involved ten or twenty men walking alongside the boat on the shore, pulling it with ropes. Next was warping, which had a few men row up in a small rowboat so that a rope could be tied to a tree, attached to the keelboat, and then the men would pull it forward through the current. Then there was poling, which had the men stand on the boats with long poles, pushing off the bottom of the river so the boat moved forward. After that there was rowing, which was the most hated method, and involved the men paddling against the current, making little headway most of the time it seemed. Finally there was sailing, which was the rarest of all keelboat travel, but came up every once in awhile when the wind was right and the boats could move along with it. Colter had done them all with the Captains, and each had their drawbacks. With cordelling you had to walk through the thick brush along shore, and sometimes in the muck and over rocks, always looking over your shoulder, wondering if an Indian might attack. Warping often left your arms feeling like they'd come out of their sockets, so much pulling on the boat was there. Poling did the shoulders in while rowing just created resentment at the one who'd ordered it. Even sailing had its drawbacks, such as when the boat suddenly veered off into an eddy or a shoal or even the bank. It was hard work, and that's why Manuel had so many men with him, just to transport the goods they'd need to make it a winter in the wilderness.

They had the goods, but little of it was food. That's one of the reasons the men had been happy to run into Colter, for they all knew from the tales George had told how good of a hunter the mountain man was. The men needed a good hunter, for they were terribly low on food by that point. They'd travelled light from St. Louis, figuring the hunting would be enough to see them through the long river voyage. Unfortunately it wasn't, with game so thin before the Platte River. Colter ran into them in late-spring and even he had a hard time finding game so that by July they were down to a quarter pound of meat per man a day. George gave them the reason for their quandary soon enough – they were travelling through Sioux Indian country, and the Indians would have already taken the plum picks. *All* the picks from what they saw.

It was with quite a bit of relief, therefore, that they made it upriver that month, reaching the Niobrara where game became plentiful. Colter's gun became quite handy by that point, and the men were quite thankful for his presence as the August days wore on.

2. THE ARIKARA

Those August days changed to September days and the men were still moving up the river, making a slow go of it. A large part of it was the hunting they had to undertake, largely to replenish the food stores. Another was the river, and the endless current that worked against them day in and day out, and during the nighttime too. Lastly it was Indians. The men had come into the territory of the "Rees," as they called the Arikara Indians, and that meant they had to keep their guard up. The Arikara village would be the first that travelers would see on their route northward on the Missouri. It was 1,440 miles from St. Louis, and Colter knew that the distance was up when he saw the village's palisade of cedar logs poking up above the riverbanks further ahead, as well as cultivated fields beginning to show nearby.

The mountain man tensed up. He'd been lucky over the rest of the winter, not seeing anymore Arikara coming after him. He'd been surprised to see them so far afield from their villages, but they'd been hunting him...for whatever reason. Colter wasn't happy he'd had to kill them all, and he expected that this had made quite a dent in the tribe's hierarchy. The Indian that'd come out of nowhere to take down the medicine man – Colter was positive only a medicine man would be wearing the get-up he'd had on – had been the ultimate surprise. Who the man was, what his importance was in the tribe, or what the problem had been between the two, Colter hadn't a clue. He'd known right away, however, that he'd still have to get past the Arikara villages further downriver, and the problem had vexed him most of the rest of the winter and into spring. After all, there was no way he could get the 400 to 500 pounds of fur he had overland, not without horses. And he wasn't about to lose anymore furs to the A'anninen for horses!

In the end he'd overcome the problem like he overcame most – charging head on in and chancing it. Colter had chosen a dark night, one with no moon or as close to it as he could get, to glide past the village. It'd taken two nights of waiting for the right time, but he'd been glad for it – the Arikara had had a large celebration on his second night, one with much whooping and dancing and drum beating, and fires too large and revealing for him to slip by. He knew they'd be worn out come the following night, however, and sure enough, they were. Moving past the village had been easy, especially with the current carrying him swiftly. After that it had been smooth sailing, quite literally with the sail that Colter had fashioned. It didn't work all the time, but it worked enough.

Now here he was, though, coming back on the Arikara and in full daylight. Whatever had happened over the winter, and whether he was still a target in the tribe's eyes, would be decided, he was sure.

"What do you think, John?" George said from the front of their boat. He had his leg propped up on a barrel and was leaning on his knee, looking at the approaching village.

"Don't know what to think," Colter said. "I snuck past at night – didn't want no trouble from this tribe."

"Well, looks like they want something from us," Manuel said, coming up behind Colter and then continuing on to the front of the boat. He pointed ahead, and it was clear that the Arikara had seen them. Braves were gathering on the shore, many armed with bow and arrows, and even a few with rudimentary muskets, guns that were far inferior to Manuel's impressive "Brown Bess."

"Must be close to a hundred already," George said, and Colter saw that it was true, and that the number was likely to grow even larger. Women and children were gathering now, as well as the old men.

"There!" Colter said as he pointed out one brave with a musket, who just then raised it up and fired off a shot into the air.

At the front of the boat George and Manuel looked at one another and frowned. The whole tribe was coming out, and it was clear the two were growing nervous. Colter began to grow nervous as well. It didn't last long, for Manuel turned about and nodded at a few of the men standing on the boat's upraised stern.

"Show 'em what we got, boys!" he shouted, and the men nodded before pulling the tarp from the swivel gun mounted there. The gun was more cannon, just a long barrel mounted on the deck with a guide handle to point it where you wanted. It was loaded with sixteen musket balls, more than enough to deliver a deadly spray to a certain area. The way the Arikara were bunched up on the shore, Colter knew that one shot would likely take out a dozen of the Indians, maybe more.

"Don't appear to be fazing them, sir," one of the men at the gun said, Jacob Reznnor Colter saw. At the boat's front, George nodded.

"They're too many in number to be cowed," he said to Manuel, and the Spaniard nodded.

"Prepare a warning shot," he called back to the men, and Colter saw the three men at the gun nod. Jacob took charge and swiveled it about so that it was pointing toward the shore, yet angled up high. Ahead of him, Manuel raised up his arm, held it for a few moments as the crowd of Indians swelled – Colter put it at around 300 now – then in one swift motion he brought his arm down, shouting "fire!"

BOOM!

The swivel gun fired to life and sent an echoing shudder through Colter. From the crowd of Indians it elicited a gasp, and more than half the huge throng turned and ran.

"Woo-hoo!" Jacob shouted. "That got 'em!"

It sure did, Colter saw. Half the tribe was suddenly gone, rushing up the banks and back to the village. Many weren't, however, and it's then that the mountain man saw the feathered headdress of what could only be the Arikara chief. The man was surrounded by armed braves, but he was waving his arm, as if inviting the men ashore.

"Steer us to shore," Manuel said, looking to the boat's pilot, John Hoback, "but just close enough for me to jump off – I want you heading back up that river and the boat behind you as well." He looked over to John Collins standing by the cabin. "Get me some of the trade gifts."

"What about you?" George said as Collins headed for the gifts. He was clearly surprised by the Spaniard's sudden change of course.

"Peter will wait for me – he's the least full of provisions and supplies," he said, referring to Peter

Weiser who was piloting their last boat. Manuel smiled and looked from George to Colter and then back again. "Relax, will you. I'm only going to be a few minutes, just long enough to talk with the chief, let him know our intentions, *and* gather as much information as I can."

"I don't like it," George said after letting out a sigh.

"I'm not paying you to like it," the Spaniard said just before Collins gave him a bundle of gifts and he jumped off the boat and into the shallow water, "I'm paying you to take orders – now go."

And with that he was trudging ashore, toward the small knot of Arikara braves that still remained, as well as the ostentatious chief that was standing amongst them. Colter watched him head ashore and toward the village, and he hoped that the Spaniard knew what he was doing. He also hoped the man's promise about getting information held true. No one wanted to know what the actions of last winter had brought the Arikara tribe more than he.

3. FIRE ON THE WATER

The Upper Missouri twisted and bent but kept up its northern course, though the current flowed south and the wind was blowing that way too. The men were making slow progress, poling themselves along. They took turns, two men on each side of the keelboat, shoving their poles down to the river bottom and pushing off, walking forward as they did so, until reaching the front of the boat, whereupon they turned about and walked back and started it all again. A man could do that for about an hour before his arms gave out, but Manuel usually relegated them to half that. He wasn't around at the moment, however, so the men were enjoying half that again. George and Colter weren't two of them, and the two Lewis and Clark Expedition veterans kept glancing back over their shoulders nervously.

"Shoulda been here by now," George said as they came upon another slight bend in the river, "shoulda been past that village by now, and well within seeing distance of us." They were on the shorter keelboat, the supply boat ahead of them now.

"Maybe the Rees weren't as friendly as he supposed," Colter said with a shrug. "Sure weren't last winter when I ran into a small band out around the Yellowstone."

"Must have been Blackfeet," George said without taking his eyes from the river behind them.

"No, they were Arikara alright, and must have been having some kind of feud between themselves for–"

"There!" George shouted out, cutting off the mountain man's words. "There he is!"

Colter spun about and sure enough, quite a ways back and just then coming around a cliff-side bend in the river, was Manuel's keelboat, the one that'd been taking up the rear behind the large supply boat.

"Looks like he made it after all," George said with a laugh, then looked over at Colter with smile. "What was all this nonsense about the Arikara last winter, huh? I bet..."

George trailed off and the smile on his face was replaced by a frown. The half-Shawnee in him had heard or sensed something, and a moment later that was clear. Shouting erupted up ahead on the supply boat and the two trappers looked up to see the men hustling about, pointing off into the thick brush obscuring the bank.

"What the hell is it?" Colter said, but a moment later he knew, for an arrow sailed out in answer and embedded itself into the gunwale near their feet. More arrows flew out, and there was even a musket shot or two, all accompanied by whooping and shouting.

Colter looked back at George, and the scout seemed to have read his mind when he said, "Damn Manuel

Lisa – how'd we ever think he wouldn't piss off the Indians?"

~~~

As the mountain man and the scout cursed their luck at being thrown in with the shady businessman, further down the river and coming around the bend was the source of their frustration. Manuel Lisa hadn't been around that long and hadn't gotten this far West without getting into a scrape or two...and having gotten out of them as well. He meant to do the same now, for he'd left the Arikara on good terms. He'd also left with quite a bit of information, one tidbit being the split that'd occurred in the tribe over the spring when it was clear some leading chieftains were *not* returning from some hunting mission. That small faction of the tribe was what he guessed was assailing them now, and he only hoped his fifty-two men could hold them off.

"C'mon!" he shouted out to the men poling the fifty-foot keelboat up the river. "Put your backs into it men – get us up to that fight!"

~~~

"Woo-hoo!" John Potts shouted out. "Got me one!"

Colter looked over at the private that'd accompanied him to the Pacific with Lewis and Clark and smiled, then reached over and clapped the German on the back. "Good, now steady yourself, reload, and get another."

Potts looked over at Colter and nodded and started to do just that, putting the butt of his rifle down on the deck, getting his ball, powder, and patch, and then ramming them all down before bringing the gun up to prime the pan and fire another shot. Seventeen seconds later Potts was shouting "woo-hoo" again.

Colter took aim with his own gun and got another himself. The Arikara were numerous along the bank now, and he suspected there were fifty of them. Most were armed with bows and arrows, others with spears or tomahawks. So far none had swum out into the river toward them, but Colter suspected that might change if they grew desperate. A glance around a moment before had told him that none of the men on the boats had been hit, but by the looks of the bodies on the river's bank, at least a dozen of the Indians had gone down, maybe more. The men were doing a good job of it, for each was an experienced rifleman. Besides Potts, there was also Peter Weiser, John Collins, and George Shannon on Colter's boat, all alumni of the voyages with the Captains. Up ahead on the large supply boat was Pierre Cruzatte, who despite the bad eyes – or eye, Colter reminded himself, for the man only had one – he'd been employed by Manuel to go back up the river. Colter hoped the man didn't shoot any of them in the backside like he'd done with Captain Lewis. Also from the expedition were George Gibson, Hugh Hall, Joseph Whitehouse, and Nathaniel Pryor. Manuel had done well recruiting the men in St. Louis at expedition's end it seemed, though the highest ranking of them, Sergeant Pryor, was still in St. Louis or somewhere hundreds of miles behind them on the river, bringing Chief Big White back up to the Mandans, fulfilling the terms of the agreement the Captains had made before sending the chief downriver and then to Washington back in 1806.

THUNK!

Colter's thoughts were interrupted, as was his aim, when a tomahawk slammed into the wooden beam right next to his head. George looked over at him with wide eyes.

"That was close!" the scout said. "Maybe we should signal up to the lead boat to open up with that swivel gun, eh?"

"Do you think?" Colter said with a scowl as he moved away from the tomahawk, which had several large eagle feathers dangling from its handle. He took up position a few feet away and took aim once again, taking out a particularly nasty looking Arikara brave that was ready to hurl yet another of the axes.

George just shrugged and headed up to the front of the boat, put his hands to his mouth, and shouted out for the men to open up with the swivel gun. Two men including Jacob had been standing beside the gun waiting to do just that, and right as they took the covering off of it a great gasp went up from the attacking Arikara. They'd seen what it could do at the villages earlier, after all. Within moments they were rushing back into the thick brush and trees, leaving their dead to litter the bank. A few minutes after that Manuel had caught up to them, and the last of the Indians had fled.

"What the hell happened back there?" George shouted out once the Spaniard was within earshot.

Manuel frowned, but then shrugged. He told them what he'd heard of the missing tribal members, and the subsequent breakdown. Both he and George looked to Colter, for they'd heard the mountain man's story of winter adventure, but hadn't believed it. Now they were beginning to wonder.

For Colter's part, he just counted the bodies as the shore receded into the distance now that the three boats were moving again. Eighteen he counted, eighteen more dead Arikara braves. He shook his head and scoffed before turning away. He knew if the whites kept this up there'd be a war with the tribe one day.

4. THE MANDAN

The Mandan village was further upriver and the men reached its outskirts a day after the Arikara attack. First came Fort Mandan, or at least what was left of it. When the men of the Captains' expedition had come back through in 1806 it'd been burned to the ground, though the Mandan could give no cause. All that'd been left when Colter had seen it was a charred spot where the large cottonwood walls and structures had once stood. Coming back down earlier this year there'd been even less, for the banks had eroded substantially and the area made all but unrecognizable over the previous winter. Colter knew the spot, however, and knew that when they reached it the first village, called Mitutanka, wouldn't be far ahead.

The Missouri opened up a bit here, forming a wide bend, almost a small lake it was so large. That's where Chief Sheheke, or Big White as Colter had sometimes heard him called, was leader. He was a big man, and that's how the men of the expedition had remembered him. Across the river and after the large bend was the second Mandan village, called Ruptare. The chief there was Black Cat. The Indians had become so numerous over the years that they'd had to split into smaller villages, lest they begin warring with themselves. Considering the outside threats from the Blackfeet to the north and west and Arikara to the south, this wouldn't have been ideal. So they expanded, and as the Missouri broke off into some offshoots, the third village of Mahawha appeared. That was led by White Buffalo, Colter knew, and a short distance upriver was the last village, called Metaharta, which was ruled by Black Moccasin. At that point the villages became much more Hidatsa as one moved upriver, for the two tribes were like brothers, the mountain man knew. There were five villages in all making up the cluster of Mandan Villages, the last being Menetarra, which was wholly Hidatsa Indian. Colter thought about the many times he'd passed by on the river, and the winter he'd spent walking through these villages. They were nearing the first, and Manuel was getting ready to go ashore, once again to pay his respects, often through gifts more than just words. It was a practice he'd picked up on his earlier Santa Fe expedition, one he preferred not to talk about. Most knew that was because it'd failed.

"Try not to rile 'em up this time," George said to Manuel with a smile as the Spaniard was packing his gift bags. He'd walk through all five villages, Colter knew, by himself, while the three boats kept up their slow pace. All the men knew that there was nothing to fear from the Mandan, for this was the tribe that the whites had traded with the most, secured the most treaty rights with, and depended upon the most for their westward expansion along the Upper Missouri. Without the Mandan, Colter knew, the whites would have a hard go of it, and probably wouldn't have been able to put down roots in the wilds here for another decade at least, maybe two.

Manuel smiled at George and shook his head. "As long as there's no Arikara visiting, I think we'll be alright."

Nearby, Potts laughed. "Mandan wouldn't let an Arikara within 400 yards of these villages, or however far one of their arrows can travel."

"About 200," George said with a frown, "you should know that."

The German gave his own frown to that and skulked away to the other side of the deck, much to the amusement of the three leading men standing there weighing their options.

"Well men," Manuel said when he'd cinched up the last of his bags, "same routine: follow me upriver and I'll do the tradin', talkin', and gettin' of information." The men nodded as the small rowboat was lowered down to the water by Edward Rose, the mulatto interpreter that that'd lived with the Osage Indians for a time before Manuel had recruited him for their voyage. He'd just be rowing the boat, for the Spaniard spoke enough Mandan and the Indians enough English and French for them to get by.

"Remember," he said before he hopped over the gunwales and into the rowboat, "this is our last stop before switching over to the Yellowstone and leaving civilization behind. Let's not dally, alright?"

Both Colter and George nodded, knowing that Manuel was talking of the men and their propensity to sleep with the native women. This'd be there last chance all winter most likely, and with Manuel walking the several miles through the villages, taking his time at each for show and gifts and talk, the men would have ample time for their own form of 'gift giving.' Any advances they still had from Manuel would likely not make it past that fifth village, still a couple hours upriver. The mountain man and the scout looked at one another and chuckled. Didn't much matter to them what the men did, so long as those boats kept moving upriver, closer to the beaver, and the money the animals brought.

~~~

The Mandans had a light complexion much different from most Indians of the region and brown hair that many thought resembled the Welsh. Some thought them a lost band of the Welsh, and that was just fine with the men from the boats. The lead keelboat was doing a good job rowing far ahead, the better to drop one man here and another man there. They were quickly beckoned into awaiting lodges, tepees, or even out of the way bushes and copses of trees. There was lovemaking to be had for them, and trade items for the women. There was a reason the Mandan were one of the largest and wealthiest tribes on the Upper Missouri, and their sexual appetites had a large part to do with that.

Manuel Lisa was oblivious to that all as he headed into the first village and then the second, meeting with Big White's second, Little Raven, as well as Black Cat. Everything went well, as it was expected to, though Manuel got his fair share of unwanted news.

"Guns," Black Cat said in rough English and even worse French, "you trade guns to too many!"

Manuel tried to assuage the man as much as he could, but in the end it was clear that there were problems. More and more rifles were appearing in the hands of the Mandan's enemies, primarily the Blackfeet. Manuel suspected it was the French and British to the north, two countries that had no problems sowing discord in the new American territory that President Jefferson had bought up just four years earlier. That wasn't good for the Mandan, which wasn't good for the Americans. Manuel knew that, but what could he do? His hands were tied, as he didn't have many guns to trade. All he could leave Black Cat with were promises that he'd not trade any guns to the Blackfeet or any other hostile tribes. That was what they wanted most of all, he knew, for the Blackfeet were foreigners here, a tribe that'd only arrived in the area over the past 75 years or so. They were better horseman and warriors than the sedentary tribes, however, and had quickly pushed many of the natives off the plains and into the Rocky Mountains. The chief had finally accepted Manuel's refusal, largely with the help of a heaping load of trinkets from one of the Spaniard's bags.

The next two villages were much the same, and by the time Manual reached the final village, the one wholly made up of Hidatsa, he just went through the motions and had the meeting over with quickly. The last keelboat was there waiting for him, the night already fast approaching by that point, and all he wanted to do was bed down in his bunk and not talk to another Indian for a few days.

After their afternoon with the women of the tribes, most of the other men felt exactly the same.

5. UP AROUND THE BEND

The days went by, late-summer changing to early autumn and then even into winter in some spots. There was no snow yet, but every tree on the riverbanks was now golden, yellow, orange or red. Mornings were getting awfully cold too. Autumn was in full swing and already on the way out in many places – the river held so many fallen leaves that sometimes you couldn't even see the water. The river held beaver, too, and there were many signs of the animals as the men pushed on up the Missouri. Trapping was the main activity if you weren't pushing or pulling or somehow cajoling the boat upstream. Most men were engaged in trapping, usually going out for a day or two at a time and always keeping close to the river and its offshoots, the better to catch the plum beaver and get the hides back on the boats quickly. All of that made Colter think of his own money, his take from the expedition.

The mountain man wasn't worried about the furs he'd trapped over the previous winter, either. Manuel had taken on quite a few men in St. Louis, and while most had proven quite sound and capable, one in particular had not. That was John Baptiste Bouche, a man that ate more rations than he was allowed while not doing enough work on top of it. He'd already been on Manuel's bad side for drinking up most of his advanced wages in St. Louis, and then getting thrown in jail on top of it. The Spaniard had bailed him out, and had come to regret it. When Colter appeared Bouche had taken the opportunity to plead his case for an early release, but Manuel had flatly refused, saying they needed all the men they could get where they were going. After learning of the man's temperament, however, Colter had wished the man would have been allowed to leave. He refused to do any work getting the boats upriver and constantly shirked his duties. Colter knew he would have grown fearful for his furs and the money due to him also if Manuel had allowed the man to leave. At the same time Colter knew the Spaniard had men in St. Louis that would have known Bouche and that even if all the furs *were* lost, Manuel would pay for them out of his own pocket. It hadn't come to that, and the packs that Colter had prepared were stowed away in the supply boat's cabin. His money would have to wait, though with any luck the value of furs would increase by the time he finally cashed them in. That thought had assuaged the mountain man, and now here he was, already late-autumn, the Upper Missouri nearly at its end, the Yellowstone just days away.

After the Mandan villages they'd moved past a Hidatsa village. Following that there was known to be roaming bands of Assiniboine, a tribe that shunned villages in favor of mobile travel dominated by tepees. They ranged to the northwest, where the Missouri curved to the west, allowing the Yellowstone to sprout off to move southward, eventually leaving the general area for another mountainous area that Colter didn't much know. Along the way travelers would pass through the heart of Crow country, though that bothered few as the tribe was as peaceful as could be. The Sioux, Assiniboine and Cheyenne were also present, as were the Blackfeet. Besides that, Nez Perce, Shoshone, A'anninen and Bannocks all ranged into the valley from across the Rockies, following the game that flocked there during the winter months. Far to the north were the Cree and Chippewa, two tribes allied with the Assiniboine in something called the Iron Confederacy. Colter hoped they didn't have any run-ins with them.

That's all you could hope for, the mountain man knew, that the area they were heading to would be free from hostile tribes. He knew the Blackfeet were on the western periphery of where the Yellowstone and Big Horn met, and that was the spot he'd told Manuel would prove the best for a trading fort. Colter also suspected with the trapping party's numbers the more-hostile Blackfeet would leave them be. It all depended on if they had horses, the mountain man knew, for that's where the true strength of the Blackfeet lay, with their superior horsemanship. He couldn't say the same for all the other tribes. They were getting into the edge of the Iron Confederacy's territory and the three-tribe alliance created a grouping even more powerful than the arguably most-powerful plains tribe of them all, the Blackfeet. Already the men had seen the overwhelming numbers the Assiniboine had been able to muster. It'd happened a few days before, with the tribe gathering on the shores just like the Arikara had. This time, however, they'd been as numerous as blades of grass on the plains.

Manuel had ordered the swivel guns fired in warning, and it'd done the trick. Colter wasn't sure how many other travelers would be able to say the same, or for how long. So far they hadn't seen either of the other two tribes, but it was only a matter of time. With luck the northern tribes would stay up in Canada as winter set in, but Colter knew that luck was a fickle one out here in the wilderness. Then there were the Arikara, the tribe that had given him so much trouble the winter before...for whatever reason. Colter scoffed. The tribes around here didn't need much reason, he knew – boredom was usually enough. The men called the Arikara "Rees" and knew them to be unpredictable, and that was *not* something Manuel wanted for his winter business venture, unpredictability.

The Spaniard looked worried as Colter glanced over at him sitting on the other side of the boat, and he was. He'd persuaded Pierre Menard and William Morrison to finance his expedition, and that's the only reason he'd been able to set out in April. The two Illinois investors were far removed from Manuel, but if they didn't start seeing some dividends from their investment soon it could finally be the thing that spelled disaster for the Spaniard's shady business dealings. Manuel wasn't likely to let that happen, but if an attack from hostile Indians came upon him, there'd be little he could do to stop it. So far he was doing well with his plans to monopolize the Upper Missouri River fur trade, but if the Rees attacked them before they even made it to the Yellowstone, those dreams would be gone, as well as the $16,000 worth of supplies the three keelboats held. That was a lot of money to be in debt for, and almost all the men of the trading expedition would be in the same sorry state. For as was custom – and the only way for many of them to get away from their own creditors – Manuel had loaned a good many of them a sizeable portion of their future earnings so they could settle debts and buy the necessary supplies for a year or more in the wild. It all meant they were in a sorry state, but they were in that state together. Manuel meant to capitalize on that fact, their debt and camaraderie in it, so they weren't *all* ruined...he especially.

Perhaps that's what Manuel was thinking, for a few minutes later he got up from his position on the boat, looked around, then began motioning and calling out to the men.

"Listen, men," he began, "we've got the Yellowstone coming up on us soon and–"

The Spaniard was cutoff as a rifle shot ripped through the air. It was from the south, the direction they'd come...the direction the Assiniboine would come from if they'd decided to come after the whites. Colter figured many of the men were thinking that, for they looked around nervously at one another. He and the other hunters were up now, rifles in hand, waiting. Something would come at them, that was certain.

Moments passed like that, then minutes. The men poling the boats slacked off and they lost ground, at exactly the time they didn't need to. But what could you do when everyone's attention was trained on the south, where the rifle shot had come from?

"Could be George," John Potts said after several minutes had gone by.

"Could be," Manual agreed, though he kept chewing his lip while looking southward. It was clear he was nervous, both for the Assiniboine, and for what Potts had said. After all, he'd sent George out with the instructions, "dead or alive." It'd all started when–

"There!" John Collins shouted out from his spot on the boat as he pointed toward the thick bushes and small trees crowding the shore. Everyone's attention shot that way, and a moment later they all relaxed, for there was George Drouillard coming through the brush, rifle in hand, distinctive yellow cap showing.

"Was that you, George?" Manuel called out, and a

moment later George nodded, raising his rifle up at the same time. The Spaniard looked to the polers and nodded. "Ease off."

The men did so, and soon they were floating downstream with the current. Once near the scout they put their poles back down and moved the boats close to shore, anchoring them against the flowing water with brute force and sheer will. Manuel didn't waste anytime once they were there.

"Did you get him?" he asked, leaning in eagerly to better hear the man's answer.

George nodded. "I shot him, but he didn't die. Truth be told, sir, I wish I hadn't."

Manuel leaned back, and Colter noticed a slight smile crease up on one side of the Spaniard's mouth, but just for a moment. "You did the right thing," he said, "now...where is he?"

"Quite a ways back, in some brush and bleedin' bad," George said as he nodded over his shoulder. "I was hoping a couple men could help me bring him back to the boats...maybe we could get him downriver, perhaps to the Mandans for help."

The Spaniard frowned to that, but a moment later he nodded and looked over at the men in the boat with him. "Two of you go with him and bring Bissonette back."

Manuel looked back to George and looked to the men. They all looked at one another until Colter let out a sigh and stepped forward. Without a word he jumped off the boat into the shallows of the river, already frigid despite the warm sun overhead, and trudged to shore. He heard a splash behind him a few moments later, but didn't need to look back to know that it was the German, Potts, that was following him. They'd been talking quite a bit since leaving the Indian villages, and had a lot in common. Turning around when he reached the shore told him he'd been correct, for there Potts was, that blond hair and those blue eyes making it plain which country he hailed from.

"Let's go," George said when Potts was ashore, the sorrow in his voice evident. The three started off.

~~~

"There he is," George said. They were about a mile from the boats and the scout was pointing to some trees standing out from a larger copse. Colter put his hand up to block out the sun, and sure enough, there was the French trapper. He'd joined on in St. Louis and had been nearly as bad as Bouche had been. The problem was that he'd had more gall than Bouche, and backed up his words with actions. Or back them up without, in this case, for the man had been smart enough to take off without telling anyone. Clearly he hadn't wanted to be in Indian country, for he'd deserted two days earlier, just a short time after the Assiniboine show of force. He'd taken some blankets and other goods with him, and anxious to assert discipline and his authority, Manuel had sent out George, their scout and crack-shot. Bissonette hadn't stood a chance.

"Damn," Potts said after they'd covered the distance to the spot where Bissonette lay dying, "shot him right in the back." It was true, Colter saw, for the trapper was lying on his stomach, his shirt a bloody mess and pooling around him. Both men looked to George.

"I didn't want to," the scout said, on the verge of tears it looked like, "but you know how Manuel gets."

Both men nodded to that. The Spaniard could be a hard driver of men, and when he thought his authority was in question, he clamped down. Colter imagined that he thought of himself as a ship's captain, always looking for mutinies and ways to suppress them. Unfortunately, George had gotten caught up in that. Both Colter and George were spared the worst of Manuel's temper, mainly because their skills were in short supply – good shooting in George's case, and while Colter had that too, it was the mountain man's knowledge of country that really set him apart.

Potts was easing in to check Bissonette's wound. A moment later he moved up to check the man's face, and then he turned back to them and shook his head.

"Won't be needing to take him back to the Mandan villages now," the German said, "unless you want an Indian burial for him."

The three men looked at one another and frowned. This wasn't an auspicious start for their trip down the Yellowstone.

6. THE YELLOWSTONE

The three men took Bissonette's body back to the boats and together with a few others, buried him on the shore. They put up a crude stone marker, though Colter suspected it'd be blown or knocked down by spring. After that they'd headed on, poling, cordelling and warping their way up the river. Most days were easy, for the river was lower this time of year, the current less. Soon it'd start freezing in spots, and knowing this, the men put their backs into it more than usual. They started covering fifteen miles a day, making up for the time lost earlier downriver. And then, finally, they reached it – the fork in the river where the Big Horn sprouted from the Yellowstone.

The Hidatsa name was Mi tse a-da-zi and the French called the river Roche Jaune, or Yellow Rock, because of that. Colter had taken to calling it the Yellowstone, and many others were doing so still. It was 20 miles downstream from Pompey's Pillar, Colter knew, the large rock monolith that jutted from the plains and the spot that Captain Lewis had carved his name at in July 1806. It was a prime spot, being in the wintering grounds of the Crow, and with lowlands that provided amble cover. Cottonwoods and Russian-olive trees choked the banks, an added air of seclusion to the place, one that afforded a bit of protection should it be needed. They'd also supply much of the timber the men would need to build the fort. Much of that timber had shed its leaves, the cottonwoods especially, though those trees were often gnarled and twisted and didn't make for the best building. There was a fair bit of pine, fir, spruce, juniper, and aspen trees, however, and they did. All in all, there was more than enough for whatever needs the men might have.

The ground was golden as they landed the boats, owing to the tall grass being starved of water this late in the year. It blew in the wind and cast shimmering sheets across the highlands above them.

"There she is," Colter said to Manuel when the were on the bank, the other men disembarking around them, looking at the location of their winter home, "this is where the fort should be."

The mountain man cast his arm out and in the minds of the men they saw the wood go up, the tar to hold it, and the gates to secure it. The fort would be situated on a wooded point between the two rivers, good timberland that would serve as both protection and source of supply. Scouting nearby had revealed that there were low-grade coal sources, something that would provide amble heat during the winter. Colter knew that the area would flood during spring and then again in summer, creating an island where the fort stood. There was more than enough room so he wasn't worried about it, and had spoken at length about it with Manuel. The Spaniard had been swayed more than anything when the mountain man had pointed out the beaver sign there, everything from huge cottonwood trees that'd been toppled, the teeth marks still showing, to the numerous dwellings that had been tunneled right into the riverbank. If Manuel had had any doubts, they'd been dispelled when Colter and George had gone up to one of the larger holes and pulled a large beaver out right then and there. He'd kicked and clawed and been mad as hell, but one bop over the head with a good club had brought them one more pelt, a $5 one by the looks of it. The final good sign had been a pair of bald eagles that'd been circling overhead ever since they'd come ashore, occasionally landing in some nearby trees. Yes, the men knew, this was the spot. Manuel seemed to know that they knew, and he was preparing himself for a speech.

Colter was eager to hear the man harangue his men. He'd heard a lot about the Spaniard, especially from Captain Lewis, who'd procured some supplies from him in St. Louis before they'd ventured out. The Captain had called Manuel a bastard, though from what Colter had since heard, it wouldn't have been the first time. Manuel Lisa was about as cutthroat as you could get when it came to a businessman. His eyes were beady and black, owing to his Spanish heritage, and his complexion was dark as well. Many suspected his business practices took on the same appearance, and they wouldn't have been far off the mark. Manuel Lisa was a man for whom the ends justified the means. Men detested and despised him, and those were the ones that'd done business with him. People were warned not to trust the man, and Manuel was known to tell people that himself, usually before entering into a business contract. Of course, the Spaniard would be the first to tell you all of those rumors were false, and just that – rumors, spread on a vast and wide frontier wilderness, the easier to reach the heights of exaggeration with. And even his firmest detractors would usually be at a loss for words when it came to explaining how the man had stayed in business all these years, if his dealings were so nefarious, corrupt, and downright rotten. More than likely it was his thrift in enterprise, firm purpose, and unstoppable energy that kept him afloat, and profitable.

Manuel Lisa stood there staring at the man, and the air grew tense. Moments passed as the man gauged which words would sink in, and Manuel let them pass. The Spaniard had grown up in New Orleans, after all, he knew what a good show was, and even out here in the wilds, thousands of miles from civilization, there was always need for show. Manuel gave it to them. He let out a long sigh, then glanced at some of the men around. George caught his eye, as did Colter. Finally he turned about, looking up toward the distant mountains to the north.

"I will build this fort," he said, his arm rising up to take in the land near the river and the area around it, "I'll build it right here. But I'll do more than that," he continued, moving about now swiftly, his arm still raised but facing the men once again. He wasn't really looking at them, however, but further up toward the mountains to the south. More than that, Colter knew, he was looking into the future.

"I'll build another fort," Manuel continued, the men's full attention upon him," and another after that and another still, all up and down the Upper Missouri and its reaches and right into the animal kingdom it represents. You, my brave trappers and hunters and scouts, it is you who I'll send out, armed and equipped, ready to do battle with them. Beaver, bear and even bison will fall to our rifles, which will be the best from Springfield, Missouri, that I promise."

There were a few laughs at the bison remark and then quite a few favorable nods at the comment on rifles. Manuel had the men in his hand and he knew it, Colter saw, though they did not. Early childhood memories of George Rogers Clark and Simon Kenton back in Kentucky came to him, and the political harangues they'd given about the British. It seemed to the mountain man that even out here in the deep wilderness, the institutions of man would follow in idea if they couldn't in fact.

There was a long pause as Manuel looked at the men around him, all fifty-one, and nodded. He'd put his rifle butt down and leaned on it as he did so, and the tension built.

"It'll be hard men, I can't lie to you there, but then I told you much the same in St. Louis. Hell, some of you know this firsthand, having lived through it with the men that came before, Captains Lewis and Clark." He nodded at George and Colter and Potts and several others. "But know that I won't put you in danger, never," he continued, and again the men nodded their assent – Manuel was telling them exactly what they wanted to hear, exactly what they *needed* to hear in order for him to remain in control out here in the wild, over the winter, and so far from the regular rule of law and requisite systems of order it was built upon. For just as a ship caught in the doldrums at sea, it's crew growing listless and bored and looking for any excuse to mutiny against their captain, so too could the mountain men and fur trappers do the same, if given the reason, excuse, and chance. Manuel was ensuring neither of those things would come about, and he was making that clear now.

"We'll build the fort and we'll build it quick," Manuel said, turning back to look at the location and the mountains that lay beyond, "for we'll need it come winter. The area largely holds friendly tribes, but as we saw coming upriver, there are others that aren't so friendly." Manuel paused again to let his words sink in, and Colter took note that the Spaniard didn't bring up the surrounding tribes' hunger for arms, whether rifle, musket or the crudest of pistols. An image of a Spanish or Italian arquebus came to the mountain man's mind and he smiled – he didn't doubt for one second that some desperate brave would instantly trade in his trusty bow and arrow for the thing, likely leading to his death as the gun no doubt misfired. The mountain man chuckled inwardly, just as Manuel began to wrap it up.

"It's the friendly tribes that we'll rely on," the Spaniard said, turning about once again, this time meeting the men's gazes firmly, and not so abstractly as before. "Those friendly tribes will supply us with the knowledge of the best trapping spots, the best hunting spots and the areas we need to stay away from come spring. Remember, the beaver toughens up over winter, and that leads to an oilier fur. The fine ladies of Paris and London and Madrid don't want *that* at their fancy balls, now do they men?"

There were laughs and shouts of "oh no" and "oh my" to that, and quite a few backs slapped as well as the rugged men let what they thought of the dandies across the ocean be known. Colter was smiling pretty widely himself.

"So we build the fort and we wait until spring, getting as many furs until winter sets in as we can," Manuel said, more seriously now. His tone caused the men to do the same, and they perked up and stood a bit straighter. Manuel didn't need to say that furs meant money, and the more a man could find, the more he'd make. It was why they were here, after all...the beauty and majesty of the land was just an added benefit. As Colter knew, it could prove to be one helluva curse.

"Well men," Manuel said at last, clapping his hands together, "you know your jobs and why you're here – snap to it." And they did.

7. FORT RAYMOND

Living out in the wilderness wasn't for everyone, and as the days passed and the fort began to take shape, the wide variety of men now calling the location home took the change differently. Colter knew that the military men among them would do the best, for they'd been put through such rigors before, spending time in forts back East. It was the new men, those that came on in St. Louis, many having come up in Tennessee and Kentucky and the territories that bordered them, that might take it the hardest. These were men like Bouche, who never went an hour without complaining about something, and not a day without doing less than everyone else. Edward Rose was becoming a pain to Manuel as well, the mountain man saw, for the man just wanted to get out and explore, he didn't want to do any work. It was work that was required, and most did their part willingly.

Colter took it all in stride, most days going out to hunt. Getting through a winter in the wilds was no easy thing he knew, and Colter had done it once with the Mandans and once one the Pacific coast before doing it solo or near enough just a few months before. Something told him he'd be doing another solo winter as well. His opinion was affirmed a couple days later when Manuel came up to him one day after he'd come back from some trapping.

"Days are growing shorter, John," he said in that southern accent of his, the rich flavors of New Orleans coming off his tongue. The mountain man only nodded before looking out at the landscape, so Manuel continued. "Won't be much for you to do here soon."

"Suppose not," Colter said.

"I've already spoken with George," Manuel said, shifting a bit and then turning to look back at the village. His tone changed too, from one that was more asking to more telling.

"Oh, about what?" Colter said, his interest now piqued.

"He wants to go out, scouting and charting the area around the Big Horn and further east."

"And what do you think?"

"I think it's a good idea," Manuel said as he turned back to look at Colter, "and I also think it's a good idea you do the same."

"With George?" Colter said, surprise in his voice. He doubted the half-Indian scout would want him tagging along, announcing their presence a mile-off for all the unfriendly tribes to hear.

"No, in the other direction – south on the Yellowstone and then overland, charting the mountains and what passes may lay between them."

There was a long pause as Manuel looked at Colter, and finally the mountain man scoffed and said, "why?"

"Because we need to move further south, we *will* move further south," Manuel said. "We need the trade with the Indians, and the friendly relations that'll bring. Already the British and French are crowding in on us and in Washington Dearborn does nothing at the War Department and Jefferson lets him get away with it." He shook his head. "I'll tell you, John, unless we get a firm border with the British to the north, there'll be war here, there's just too much money at stake."

Colter let the words sink in for a moment before turning around to look at the Yellowstone behind him, the one he'd just come from and the one he'd spent so much time on as of late. Manuel was telling him to go back to that river, yet farther afield as well. Out into the wild really, the unknown, and with no way to know what would be out there. Colter had already seen some strange things, had encountered some strange characters. He didn't know if he wanted to see anymore.

"You'll be going it alone," Manuel said after Colter had been staring at the river for awhile, coming up to stand beside the mountain man, "at least until you get into Crow country."

"Oh?" Colter said, turning to face him. That *did* surprise him.

Manuel nodded. "The Crow have already agreed to guide you south, through the pass between the Absarokas and the Wind River Range and then back up to the Yellowstone from the other side, at least that's what I was told at the Mandan villages. They want trade, need it bad in fact, in the face of the Iron Confederacy's grip on the waterways to the west of them."

"I see you've been planning, Manuel," Colter said.

The Spaniard smiled. "Always."

He gave Colter a clap on the back and then started to walk back to the fort, calling over his shoulder, "think about it, John, think about it."

Colter kneeled down on the rocky shore of the river and chewed his lip. He would think about it, but not for long. He didn't need to.

8. AROUND THE FIRE

The fire crackled and popped and shot embers soaring into the night sky. Up above were Orion the hunter and Gemini the twins, two constellations of many that touched the edges of the Milky Way Galaxy looking down. Colter traced them in his mind's eye and remembered the nights the captains had explained them, and the many nights he'd seen others just like them, both on the expedition and on his own.

The mountain man looked around at his companions, men that were hard at work building Fort Raymond, gathering winter stores, and of course trapping beaver on both the Yellowstone and the Big Horn. It was night now, however, and a special one at that – Colter and George would be leaving in the morning, each heading off in different directions, each tasked with opening up trade with the Indians. They'd taken too long coming up the river, both because of the earlier incident with Bissonette and the trouble with the Indians on the way. Colter supposed it wasn't so much trouble as time – the tribes all expected shows of respect and the giving of many gifts. The troublesome tribes usually took the least amount of time to impress, or cow, depending on how you wanted to look at it. Colter knew that the Missouri River was truly to blame for the winding waters were difficult to traverse, especially when you were trying to push three keelboats up it, literally. All the men around the fire that night were well-muscled and fine specimens of what a hard day's work could bring.

Around the fire that night were the whole lot of them, all wishing the two explorers well. Manuel had also loosened up with the fort's alcohol stores, which weren't plentiful and now flowed freely, or at least as free as the men's advanced wages allowed. Edward Robinson was playing the fiddle and Potts was drumming along in time. The men were pretty good, or at least the alcohol was, for John Hoback, Jacob Reznor, and Francoise LeCompt were all dancing and clapping and having a good 'ol time. LeCompt was a half-blood trader that was almost as good at tracking as George, and Colter figured he'd be put to good use over the winter, finding game for the hunters. Edward Rose would probably be at his side, the mountain man knew as he looked over at the mulatto, or half-white half-negro that'd served as an interpreter while living with the Osage Indians around St. Louis, for the man was also a good tracker. The men who weren't would be doing tasks around the fort, and they were happy to be away from them that night. They included John Collins, Pierre Cruzatte, George Gibson, Hugh Hall, and Joseph Whitehouse. All had been privates along with Colter on the expedition with the Captains, and all were a bit saddened to see Colter leave their midst so soon again. There were forty-one others just like them gathered round the fire, many unknown to Colter save through small bits of conversation here and there. There were two others that weren't present – Nathaniel Pryor and George Shannon – and Colter wondered how their quest to get Chief Big White back to the Mandan Villages was going. Supposedly they'd been having a helluva time of it, something that irked Captain Clark to no end it seemed.

All those thoughts were of little concern to Colter and George, two men on the edge of freedom, tasting it, and eager to dive right on in. The other men knew it, and they did much to change the subject, speaking of things closer to the fort, mainly so they'd be able to stay there and not wander off. The men discussed the area they were in and the problems they might face. The winter was viewed as the greatest hazard, for a man caught alone in the elements wouldn't stand a chance for long, what with the wind causing temperatures of fifty below at times. The surrounding tribes were another. Manuel didn't much figure the Assiniboine would try anything, not after the show on the river several weeks before with the swivel guns, but the Blackfeet were another matter. All the men knew of the run-in the small group led by Captain Lewis had had back in July 1806, and since then there'd been no contact with that tribe. They were out there, however, and it was likely that Colter, heading west, would encounter some of them. He hoped not, and he hoped the Crow contingent he was to travel with would offer at least a modicum of protection. All the mountain man could do was wait and see and hope that he found them soon after leaving the fort.

Manuel came up to Colter and sat down, passed a bottle over, and stared into the fire. Colter had a healthy drink before handing it back, and then the Spaniard had one himself.

"I want you to ask about Francois-Antoine Larocque," he said after a few moments had passed.

"Larocque?" Colter said. "The Frenchman that wintered with the captains and us at Fort Mandan?"

Manuel nodded. "He headed back up to Fort Montagne La Bosse on the Assiniboine River after that, but I know from talking with the Mandan that he was back that June, trading again, and this time moving further south as well, down the Big Horn." He nodded his head at the distant river, still audible at night and in the darkness, a constant droning rush that always let the men know that travel and business and danger were close at hand.

"What interest do you have in a Canadian North West Company trader?" Colter asked after a moment.

"He visited the area with a group of Crow in September 1805, a full year before your Captain Clark had been in the area."

Colter narrowed his eyes. "I wasn't aware of that."

"Most aren't" Manuel said with a nod and a smile. "What it means for us is that a white has already ventured where you're to go, opened up relations, perhaps stumbled into dangerous situations...all so you don't have to."

Colter shrugged – there was that, but one thought couldn't leave his mind. "What happened to him?"

The Spaniard frowned. Larocque had told the Crow he wanted bear and beaver furs and would trade with them until their heart's content. As far as anyone knew, the Frenchman had not yet returned. The Crow Indians knew full-well the predilection for furs among the whites, and they'd already built up a good supply to trade with the men. What had happened with the Frenchman might not be that important to them, but for Manuel it was. Information was more valuable than currency at times in the wild, and there were few whites about. Regardless of nationality or business affiliations, those men were out there in the elements, out of their *own* element, and they had to look out for one another. The Spaniard knew without a doubt that it could be *he* that went missing tomorrow, just as the Frenchman had done some time ago. Finally Manuel answered the mountain man's question.

"No one's sure, but it's supposed he died out there sometime in 1806 – no one ever heard from him after he left the far-northern fort, at least not any whites."

"Well, then the Blackfeet most likely got him."

Manuel nodded. "Most likely, but I want you to ask around, especially with the various Crow villages you come across. Tribes talk, even when they're at war, and news of a lone white travelling in the wilds wouldn't have stayed secret for long."

"Unless he just up and had enough of it and got on the river and headed back to civilization," Colter said, thinking of Joe Dixon all the while. Colter hoped the trapper he'd been with for a few months had made it back to St. Louis alright, but he had no way to know.

"Could be," Manuel said, but if so, he'd likely have travelled back up north and taken the Ottawa River east to Montreal. As he should – the French don't belong here anymore, this land is America's now."

"That may be," Colter said at last, knowing the conversation was near its end when Manuel pulled out his bottle and passed it over for Colter to enjoy a bit more of.

As he took that drink of whiskey he couldn't help but think of the river that they were on and all the others he'd pass by over his winter alone. It was late in the season and hunting and trading opportunities had been missed, so there really wasn't much for him to do around the fort. The wilds it was then, another solo-trek out there were few if any whites had been before. The thought warmed the mountain man more than the whisky, and once again he let his thoughts wander as the fire crackled and popped and he looked up at Orion and Gemini above.

9. THE BLACKFEET

The fires crackled and the sparks flew up into the night sky, but no one heard nor saw them, so intent was their focus on the drumming. Dozens of Blackfoot braves were gathered around the fires, beating their drums, creating a cacophony of sound, inviting the warrior spirits to them. That's what Chief He Who Shouts said ought to happen, after all, and he was right.

BOOM BA-BOOM BA-BOOM!

Wolf Calf looked over at the tribe's leader. Chief He Who Shouts was the only chief the young brave had ever known, was the only chief *most* of the Piegan Blackfeet tribe had ever known. He'd been ruling over the tribe for more than 30 years, though some of the older women sometimes hinted that he'd had a hard time coming about his position. He was old and wise and quiet now, more apt to listen than to shout, but in his younger days he'd earned his name well, so critical had he been of his elders. Now *he* was the elder, and it was up to others to be critical of him. Those others were the Wise Ones, and currently the tribe had three. They were Silver Heart, Buffalo Child, and Stone Bear. Each had their own unique characteristics and their own way of ruling their bands of warriors. Each also knew that they would make the best chief, when He Who Shouts finally passed on to Above World...*if* he ever passed on. Many wondered if he ever would, and not a month went by anymore without some of the younger braves talking about their chief's younger days, and what he'd seen when he'd been out in the wilds. Some said he'd come face to face with the Sky People, others said he'd gone up to Above World himself. Perhaps most fanciful of all were the tales that had him fighting Manitoin, the hairy man of the mountains that chilled even the most hardened warrior to *his* bones.

BOOM BA-BOOM BA-BOOM!

Wolf Calf stared up at Chief He Who Shouts and wondered how those tales could even have started. The chief of the Blackfeet was old and decrepit and ready to die. Wolf Calf hoped he would die, and soon, the better for his own father, Stone Bear, to take over the top spot. He was a Wise One, after all, though even Wolf Calf had to admit that his father's chances at the top spot were probably the lowest of all the three Wise Ones. Still, they were much better than the previous leader of the Skunk Band's had been. River's Kiss had led the Skunk Band before Stone Bear had taken over, and the warrior had been old and cautious. During his last few years the Skunk Band had lost steadily more ground to the other bands in the tribe, even some of their fellow Blackfeet tribes, the Piegan and the Blood. That'd all changed when Stone Bear had come to power over the previous winter. While some said the circumstances were a bit mysterious, and that River's Kiss had still been in good health when he passed on, Wolf Calf knew that no matter *how* his father had come to power, it was the best thing for the Skunk Band. It was the best thing for him.

BOOM BA-BOOM BA-BOOM!

As if reading his thoughts, Stone Bear glanced over, met his son's eyes for a moment, and nodded. Wolf Calf was filled with an immense amount of pride, for his standing in the tribe had risen considerably the day his father had taken over the Skunk Band. It'd grown considerably more earlier that day when he'd brought back the news of the reappearance of the whites.

Earlier that day Wolf Calf had stood on a distant shore of the river, not believing his eyes. There, not more than a few hundred yards ahead of him, was a large group of whites. And unlike the whites he'd seen the year before, these appeared to be setting up a permanent camp where the two rivers met.

The young Blackfoot Indian had shaken his head and smiled despite himself. *Are they that dumb?* he'd thought. *Are they really going to come and set up in* our *territory?*

He'd shaken his head again as he'd turned around and started walking back toward his village. After what had happened last year and then over the winter, Wolf Calf knew that the chiefs of the Skunk Band of the Pikuni Tribe of the Piegan Blackfeet Nation would be interested. They'd be more than interested, the young brave had known, especially after he told them of one man in particular.

What the young brave tried not to think about were the incidents of last summer, when he'd been with his friends and had actually encountered the whites. That meeting had taken Calf Looking. It'd also brought the wrath of the Otter Band down upon him, and his father. *What were you doing so far to the west?* Wolf Calf thought to himself. *What were you doing going up to whites? What makes you think you're a warrior?*

It was that last that had stung the most, and as Wolf Calf watched the warriors drumming, he wondered how much longer he'd be called a boy and not a man. Little Mouse was never called a boy, even though he was the same age as Wolf Calf. That probably had something to do with his father being the most powerful of the three Wise Ones, the esteemed Buffalo Child, the one that all expected to take over for He Who Shouts when the time finally came. Buffalo Child led the Otter Band, and that meant that his son Little Mouse led the Otter Band among the youngest of the braves, the boys like himself. *Men,* Wolf Calf reminded himself quickly.

The Otter band was strong in the tribe, much stronger than the Skunk Band of he and his father. They'd lost power over the winter when the transition had taken place, and had lost power the previous summer as well. Losing two young braves to the whites had been costly, both in lives and in tribal politics. For Calf Looking had been the son of Silver Heart, the second most powerful of the Wise Ones, though one that didn't lead a band of his own. He had once, an offshoot of the Otter Band, but he'd disbanded it over the winter, both because of what had happened to Calf Looking and because of the events surrounding the Arikara tribe to the east, *and* their calamitous run-in with one white in particular.

BOOM BA-BOOM BA-BOOM…BOOM!

With a loud crescendo, the drumming stopped. The air was filled with silence, the sound of the fire popping, and the distant murmur of the river running. All eyes were on Chief He Who Shouts, and what he was about to say.

The old chief of the Piegan Blackfeet raised his hand up slowly then moved it over to his left, to where Stone

Bear was sitting. He nodded at the Wise One. The leader of the Skunk Band took his time, let the silence build. Slowly he stood up, turned about, let all the members of the band get a good look at him. He was tall, broad of shoulder, and short of hair. He kept it trimmed close to his head, something that accentuated those piercing brown eyes of his. Those eyes bore into the gathered braves now, for there were still doubters after all, still those that thought he *shouldn't* be the leader of the Skunk Band, should *never* have been leader. Now was his chance to silence those doubters once and for all.

"My brothers and sisters," he began, speaking slowly and a bit quietly. Those gathered around had to crane their ears, scoot a bit closer, and do everything they could to focus their attention upon Stone Bear. He wouldn't have had it any other way.

"The times are changing," he continued, and there were several nods and mumblings of assent. "The times are changing and they'll never change back to the way they were – we know that now. We know that the whites will come and they will keep on coming until they fill this land like the grasses that fill the plains. They'll push us westward, as the eastern tribes pushed the fathers of our fathers many moons ago. That means we'll push the other tribes, like we have been, and they'll resent us even more for it, as they do now." He paused, let the words sink in, let the band's confidence in him build. "So what are we to do? What are we to do in the face of this overwhelming onslaught, this unending stream of violators to our lands, and the hatred the other tribes have for us?"

"We fight!"

There were a few gasps at that, and even Wolf Calf was surprised that someone had shouted out, interrupting his father. Then he realized that everyone was looking back at him, and that it'd been he that'd shouted out the words. His face was suddenly red, though ahead of him his father smiled.

"Don't be ashamed of your zeal to do what's right," Stone Bear said with a smile, holding out his arm to point out Wolf Calf to all present, "don't be ashamed of wanting to do what's right."

Wolf Calf nodded and some of the red went from his face, *some*. Stone Bear smiled again, and continued on.

"It was Wolf Calf here, the young brave that ran across the whites last summer, that ran across them again today. He's a magnet for them, and we should thank him."

That elicited a few murmurings of surprise, and Wolf Calf's eyes narrowed as he looked around. *What was his father getting at?*

"Wolf Calf spotted the whites, was there when they killed two young members of our tribe, and was the one that rushed back to tell us of this crime. He reached us quickly, but not as quickly as the whites were able to get out of the area. By the time we'd gone back in numbers they were gone, all trace of them as well." He paused, his arms out, letting the tension build. "But they're back now, Wolf Calf has seen them, and he's seen something more." He pointed out the young brave once again. "Tell them, my son, tell them what you saw."

Wolf Calf swallowed, then rose up so that all could see him. What he had to say was important, and he wanted them to know that this was *their* moment, this was the Skunk Band's moment to shine and take their rightful place among the larger Blackfeet Nation.

"When I came across the whites last summer," the young brave said, starting out slowly, taking his cue from his father, "there were just four men. One, however, had something that I'll never forget, and that was a yellow cloth upon his head. The man was part-Indian, that much was clear, but it was that yellow head-cloth which never left me."

There were mumblings in the crowd – they'd heard this story before, many times, *too* many. Wolf Calf sensed this and got to the point.

"Today while at the fork in the rivers, I saw that yellow-cloth once again, and on the same man!" He spoke loudly, with confidence. "It's the same man that killed Calf Looking," he said, "the same that killed Sidehill Calf, the same that came into our land to do as he pleased, and now he's back to do some more." He paused, looking around much like his father would, and then let them have it. "He's come back to finish the job he's started, he's come back to kill us all! Are we going to let that happen? No! No – we're going to go out and kill him first!

BOOM BA-BOOM BA-BOOM

The drums cried out after that loud pronouncement, and there were quite a few gasps and mumblings to his words, but when Wolf Calf looked back to Chief He Who Shouts he saw that the chief was smiling. He'd done well, he knew, he'd done very well.

10. A VISION QUEST

Arapoosh reached the spot he'd chosen and came to a stop. His breath heaved and the sweat beaded off him. With hands on knees, he looked up and back the way he'd come. As he'd hoped, empty forest was all that greeted him.

He let out a sigh and rose up and started walking. It was clear no one was following him, but then why should they be? No one in the tribe much cared about "Sore Belly," as he was called. Taunted and teased was more like it. The thought of his nickname brought a frown to Arapoosh's face. He'd gotten the name because he often got startled and fell down to the ground to crawl away on his stomach. They wouldn't call him Sore Belly for long, though, Arapoosh promised himself. If anything, they'd call him "chief" one day.

That last brought a smile to his face. His brother Thrown into the Spring had always said he'd make a good chief of the River Crow, had even said it up to that night. Arapoosh kicked at a clod in the earth when he thought back on that night last winter. The sky had been so clear, and the world so inviting. It was obvious that the powers of Above World were strong that night, so the boys had gone out.

Braves, Arapoosh thought to himself, *we were braves.* They'd reached that age, after all, 13-years old when the time to leave boyhood was reached. That was also the time of the vision quests, and both brothers had been adamant about going out on their own soon, even if the tribal elders said they weren't ready.

Thrown into the Spring had said they were ready, however, so that night they'd went. For the Crow there were beings of the sky – the sun, moon, stars, clouds, and even birds – that were very powerful. Going out on a vision quest was a way to meet those beings of the sky – the Sky People of Above World – and possibly garner their favor. That could lead to supernatural powers, and the River Crow were full of such tales happening in the past. If a warrior had a vision he would draw those visions on his shield, and even attach bird feathers or bird heads. Many of the ancient shields were still treasured by the oldest of the chiefs, and Arapoosh wondered if his would be among them one day.

He glanced down at the shield, his Apsaalooke as it was called. It depicted his brother, Thrown into the Spring, just as he remembered him to be. His twin had been taken into the sky that night when the two were out, shortly after they'd seen the bright light. Arapoosh had looked everywhere for him, but after seeing a band of Blackfeet, he'd thought better of looking anymore and headed back to the village. To this day he wished he hadn't.

Thrown into the Spring had always been prized more than his brother had, and when Arapoosh showed back up at the village early the next morning without him, and only a tale that he'd been taken by those from Above World, he'd been shunned. The other members of the tribe wouldn't talk to him, his friends wouldn't see him. It was easy for the tribe to do – Arapoosh's mother had died giving birth to him and his father had died in a Blackfeet raid when he was younger. The fact that he had some Hidatsa in him also didn't help. All for the rest of the winter he'd had to fend for himself, scrambling for the tribes' scraps, no one interested in what he had to say.

The River Crow were not in a good place, and hadn't been since the last bout of pestilence that had swept through. It'd claimed their chief, and ever since then their medicine man had taken over. He was old and set in his ways, and wanted nothing to do with tales of Above World. He wanted to trade with whites for as many guns as he could, the better to fight the Blackfeet with. Arapoosh shook his head when he thought of the old man's intransigence. The Blackfeet weren't the problem, it was the ever increasing number of whites coming into their lands. But even he knew that wasn't their real problem, which was that their way of life was dying.

Arapoosh glanced down at his shield. There was his brother staring back at him, or at least the best depiction that he could make. And around the shield were crane feathers. For although Arapoosh couldn't explain it, he knew that only the cranes knew where Thrown into the Spring could be found. If the cranes had the answer, there was only one way they could deliver that to Arapoosh, and that was through a vision quest. The young River Crow Indian knew he'd find the answers there.

PART II – SOJOURN

11. FIRST MORNING

Colter had the bare essentials with him, nothing more. He was wearing the same buckskin shirt he'd worn the previous winter, though new leggings over his pants. He had a buckskin jacket to keep the wind off and for the snow he had a buffalo robe. It'd do for sleeping as well, and his pack could double as a pillow. Colter had it at thirty pounds, with salt, tobacco, trade trinkets, ammunition, and a few other supplies making up the majority. Then there was his gun, the Northwest Trade Gun. God he hoped it'd be enough, for where he was going, there were no others.

Colter stood staring down at that gun, the one that would replace the prized Kentucky Rifle he'd lost the previous winter. It was a Barnett Trade Gun, to be specific, and Colter was pleased with that at least. The guns were the best in use west of the Mississippi, and the name had been known in England for more than 300 years. It had an octagonal-shaped barrel, 36 inches in length, and fired a .54 caliber round. The brass side plate was shaped like a serpent or dragon and had two thread lock bolts passing through to the trigger guard, just missing the breech plug, to thread into the barrel tang. That trigger guard was oversized, something many figured had been done to allow a gloved or mittened hand to pull it back easier. Colter knew that the real reason was because in 1740 a Hudson Bay trapper at Fort Albany had figured out the Indians preferred a two-finger trigger as opposed to a one-finger trigger, likely because of their propensity to do the same with their bow and arrows. The stock was made out of cedar wood, and featured a long comb, the place where the butt stock merged with the wrist. All told she was 52 inches in length and could take down a bear if need be. She was a killing machine, and Colter loved her already.

It'd be the only gun the mountain man carried, and he'd have to be careful. He had three pounds of powder rationed out in two horns and plenty of ball and patches as well as an extra ramrod. He figured at sixty-five grains of powder per shot he'd have enough for 100 rounds, maybe more if he was conservative. Mainly, though, he hoped he wouldn't have to use the gun too much. Hunting would be sparse in the deep winter, he knew, though the rivers would still be teeming with trout just below the ice.

"You gonna stand there like an idiot all day or are we gonna get moving?"

Colter was startled by the words and turned about to see George standing there. Obviously he'd been daydreaming, thinking of fish in rivers and what else he might be eating over the next five months. Those thoughts were all brushed aside when he looked at his friend and fellow Lewis and Clark expedition alum. The mountain man shook his head and let out a big sigh, one loud enough for George to take note of and turn his way.

"*Again*, George?" Colter said with a frown. "Yellow again?"

George's eyes narrowed as a look of confusion came across his face, then he moved his hands up to his head when realization struck him.

"I like this color," he said, adjusting the yellow headband that covered his head and hair, "it looks good on me."

Colter scoffed. "Makes you stand out a mile away is what it does."

The scout chuckled and then waved the words away with his hand. He'd heard it all before on the expedition with the Captains, he didn't need to hear it again. Best thing to do when John Colter got to complaining, he knew, was to change the subject.

"What'd you get the pack down to?"

That brought an even larger frown to the mountain man's face, for he'd been working for the past day and most of the previous night on his pack, trying to get as much as he could, while also making it weigh as little as he could. So far he was losing, badly. His frown told as much to George, who shook his head and walked up closer to take a look at the pack at the man's feet.

"You won't be needing a lot of traps, that's for sure.

"No, but I'll need a few," Colter said, remembering what he'd used one for last winter, "you never know what you might run into out there."

"You can't carry that many furs overland, and the Crow aren't going to be carrying 'em for you, not even on a travois."

"Nope, but I'll need a fair amount of trade goods –

Manuel is adamant that I hand out as many trinkets as I can so as to build up as much goodwill as I can."

"The better to create as many profits for Manuel as possible," George said. It was clear the Spaniard and his money-grubbing ways were beginning to wear on the scout.

Colter raised an eyebrow. "Is there anything else he cares about?"

They both began to chuckle and nod to that, at least until a New Orleans-accented voice came from behind some bushes.

"I care about the safety of my men, I'll tell you that."

The mountain man and scout spun around, and both had a look of surprise on their face. There behind them was Manuel, smiling, his arms crossed in front of him and his head shaking from side to side.

"If a profit-obsessed Spaniard can sneak up on you, then what chance do you men think you've got out in the wild?" he asked.

George frowned to that, but Colter only cracked a smile and looked over at him. The half-Shawnee half-French-Canadian scout wasn't used to being snuck up on, but finally he too broke out into a smile.

"Why, I knew you were there all along, Manuel – your fingers don't stink of beaver oil, and that points you out a mile away."

The Spaniard frowned to that, for everyone knew that Manuel would do just about anything out in the wild but get his hands dirty. He let the two men have their fun for a moment, and even cracked a smile himself, though barely. After that he nodded to George.

"Got everything? You'll be out there for a good five months at least."

The scout nodded, patted a few pouches and his main bag.

"How 'bout you?" Manuel said next, looking to Colter.

"All outfitted and ready to go."

Beside him, George scoffed, and Colter narrowed his eyes before looking over. Manuel did the same, and George began to shake his head.

"Thinks he's gonna be fine with just his Northwest Trade Gun, here," George said, now making some 'clucking' sounds with his tongue.

Colter frowned as Manuel looked over at him, for now he too was shaking his head. That lasted for a second before he reached into his voluminous buffalo robe and pulled out a pistol.

"That's my Harper's Ferry 1805," he said of the gun, handing it over to the mountain man. Colter set down his musket and took the pistol, turned it over in his hands a few times. It was a flintlock, with silver fittings and a shiny golden butt plate. The trigger guard was also golden in color though the barrel was silver, with a small wooden ramrod fitting snugly under it. It was a fine pistol, and Colter raised it up and admired it from every angle while Manuel smiled. The mountain man quickly realized he had a much better weapon than the Captain's McCormick pistol from last year.

"I'll take good care of it and have it back to you in spring," Colter said, looking up to Manuel with a smile.

"You'd better," the Spaniard said with a scoff as he turned and started to walk back toward the fort, "or you'll be paying me what it cost, $5."

"$5!" Colter said, eyes going wide, and beside him George whistled.

Neither man heard what Manuel said to that, for by that time he was muttering in Creole under his breath and shaking his head all the while. The two smiled, and started out.

12. THE SHOSHONE RIVER

Colter spent the days moving through a set of mountains that rose up high on his left, to the east of him. He'd been thinking of Nathaniel Pryor when he'd first spotted them and had thought of them as the Pryor Mountains ever since. Who knows, maybe the name would stick.

Colter had moved south along the Yellowstone after leaving George a few weeks before, the scout heading east the mountain man heading west. He'd followed the river for more than a day before striking south overland. Two days of walking showed that there were some distant mountains on the horizon, and it'd taken Colter another day to reach them. The early morning mist clung to them and produced a haze that lingered, creating a melancholy sense in the man. He pressed on despite it or because of it, and was rewarded two days later when he reached a river.

It was two rivers, actually, the larger Big Horn and then a smaller branching off of it. He knew one was coming up, and what it'd be like, but nothing could have prepared him for the second, or how bad it was. The smell was God-awful and he nearly retched when he'd first inhaled a chestful. He called it the Stink Water and kept his distance from it, something that helped somewhat. He knew that some tribes called it the Shoshone River, probably on account of how much they thought that tribe stunk, but he thought his name better. The stretch of water was beautiful, there was no doubt about that, what with the mountains rising up and giving over to another, larger range that headed south by southeast, but God did it smell bad. Must be some sulphur up there, he figured.

He turned his thoughts away from that and focused on his main dilemma, and that was meeting the Crow. Manuel had been convinced that it wouldn't be a problem, but he was already several weeks out from the fort now, in their territory, and he hadn't seen one sign of them. Colter knew that he'd be running into them soon, however, and so he kept his eyes peeled. Anything could be out in these wilds, he knew...anything.

13. THE FRENCHMAN

Francois-Antoine Larocque sat on the bank of the river chewing his lip and trying to look as mean as he could. If he looked mean, he knew, the Cree would leave him alone. For the most part, that is – there were always a few young boys that were ready to push and prod him and generally make him feel like the hostage he was. The Frenchman frowned, let out a sigh, and kept right on chewing.

He was tall when not stooped over, which he was more than often as of late, being pulled or dragged somewhere it seemed. The latter had turned his clothes to rags, with more holes than he could count. They hung off him, his tattered trousers and shirt from Montreal, though his moccasins and fur coat were holding up. His hair was black and his eyes brown, and those eyes darted about constantly, always wary, always looking for trouble. He rubbed at his bristly face, for even out here in the wilds as an Indian captive he did his best to shave.

He hadn't always been an Indian captive, far from it. When he'd left Fort Montagne La Bosse on the Assiniboine River in the spring of 1805 he'd been one of the leading trappers of the North West Company. The Company still called the area the Upper Red River Department, and the surrounding Assiniboine, Souris, and Qu'Appelle Rivers were all dominated by them. Even Lake Manitoba and Like Winnipeg further north had their fingerprints all over them, and all trappers knew, the northlands belonged to the French still to this day.

The previous winter Laroque had travelled south to the Mandan Villages with fellow a trapper. There he'd met with the American explorers, Lewis and Clark. They'd been a bit gruff and not interested in him, more concerned that the Frenchman would share their secrets with the competing foreign interests in the area, so he'd cut his time there short. When the Company got wind of what the Americans were up to, however, Laroque was sent back. His boss, Charles J.B. Chaboillez, was adamant that he get down there and cement trading relations with the friendly tribes before the Americans did.

He reached the Mandan villages for the second time in Mid-June and declared his intention to trade with the neighboring Crow tribe. The Mandans were adamant that he not travel to Crow lands, for the Mandan would lose out their middle-man between the whites and the Crow. The Mandans pretended to be afraid of the other tribes – Assiniboine, Sioux, Cheyenne, and Pawnees – because they didn't want the whites selling them guns.

The Crow didn't mind, however, and things didn't work out for the Mandan chiefs when more than 600

Crow Indians arrived at the Mandan villages at the end of June. Laroque spoke with them and then at the end of the month he travelled with them to their villages. They passed the Knife, Little Missouri, and Powder Rivers further to the southwest. By mid-August they'd reached the Tongue River and then turned north to move through the Wolf Mountains. By the end of August they'd reached the Big Horn River and camped on Lime Kiln Creek.

While the Mandan were worried that the Crow and other tribes like them were only interested in guns, the truth of the matter was that they were interested in just about everything under the sun. The best items, Laroque and other trappers like him had discovered, were simple things like cock feathers, rings, beads, colored glasses, papers, and the pigment vermillion. They were also interested in items that had a bit more use, and the Frenchman always made it a point to carry quite a few small knives, large knives, awls, and ball and powder. For while he might not trade that many guns with the Indians – he didn't have that many to trade, and carrying more than a couple was quite burdensome – that didn't mean many of the Indians didn't already *have* guns, weapons that just needed ammunition. Laroque was happy to trade it with them, so long as he got the furs he was looking for. While the man knew how to bait and set a trap just as well as the next trapper, he tried to keep his hands clean as much as possible. Trading was the way to do that, and although all the items previously mentioned were fine and dandy, nothing could excite the Indians like tobacco (alcohol of course excited them much more, but Laroque had learned early on, after a particularly bad night in fact, that trading it to them did little to excite him). Tobacco was another matter entirely, for it didn't lead to violence, and the Frenchman doled it out generously wherever he went...in return for payment, of course.

He'd been doling it out quit liberally that September of 1806, so much so that he quickly became overburdened with trade goods of his own, furs and pelts mainly, though a few other Indian knick-knacks as well, for there was a growing market for such, no matter how useless the things might be. All of that had caused Laroque to head back up the Big Horn near the beginning of October. Mid-month saw him at the Mandan Villages for more trading, and then he went overland to the Souris River, was happy to see the boat he'd left was still there, undisturbed by the Chippewa Indians, and then went onward to Fort Rouge at the southern end of Lake Winnipeg. The place was pretty empty that time of year, and had been that way since the 1750s when it'd largely been abandoned. Alexander Henry "The Younger" had built it back up in 1803, however, and that meant that Larocque could winter there in relative comfort, as much as you could get out in the wilds, 1,100 miles from the nearest Canadian city of any size, Montreal. It was late-November by that point, however, and it wasn't likely that the Frenchman could make the overland journey to the city that late in the year. It would have to be overland, for the rivers were already freezing solid.

And so Larocque had waited out the winter, his sights set on heading east to Montreal come the first thaw, but those plans had been interrupted come March when two fellow Frenchmen came along one day, fresh from their winter out on the Saskatchewan and Qu'Appelle Rivers. Larocque had never seen two men so weighed down with furs, and all thoughts of heading back to civilization left him when they began calculating how much money those men had coming. A deal was struck right then and there that the two would take Larocque's haul back to Montreal, for a small cut of course, depositing it into his Bank of Montreal account there. It was a small gamble trusting the men, but the Frenchman knew that the frontier was a small place when it came to whites, and that they'd likely cross paths again. If there'd been any past improprieties, it wouldn't be a friendly shout that met the trappers, but a rifle shot, hopefully one that killed.

Laroque doubted it would come to that, and he didn't much care – thoughts of riches were going through his head as he started overland once again, heading back south to the Mandan Villages. He reached them in the spring of 1807 but so hungry for profits was he that he didn't even stop at them, in fact, kept quite a distance, picking up the Missouri further on. By May he was on the Yellowstone and then a short time later he was heading back down the Big Horn. He hadn't run into any Crows along the way, but he was hoping he would, both to trade with and to learn the best beaver spots that year. Unfortunately, it wasn't the Crow that he ran into, but the Cree.

It'd occurred around the Wind River, and was as simple as the Frenchman tearing through a small copse of trees just as a band of Cree braves was tearing through another. They'd come face to face, and for a moment both the white and the Indians paused, unsure of what to do. The Frenchman had ended that quickly when he turned and ran, hoping against hope that he could outrun the braves, perhaps lose them somewhere on the river. He was thinking just that when he glanced back over his shoulder to see how close they were on his tail, then turned back to see a large and low-hanging tree branch before him. He'd hit it, and everything had went black. When he'd come to, his hands and feet were tied and he was sitting on the edge of a fire near a river, the band of Cree carousing and enjoying his supplies, especially the small bottle of Whiskey he'd had, not to mention all of his tobacco.

Laroque frowned and let out a sigh as he thought back to the events that had brought him to his current predicament, chewing his lip all the while. It'd been six months now that he'd been a captive, and winter was setting in once again. That meant he'd be marched back to the main Cree village, a place he'd only been brought to twice before. It seemed the Indians liked having him out in the wilds with them, doing much of the hard trapping work for them. The Frenchman obliged, for he knew the alternative was death. Now that the rivers were freezing, however, the beaver toughening up for the winter, their furs becoming oilier and less sought after, Larocque knew that his value was nearing its end. In the summer he could work for his food; in the winter he'd likely be cutoff as stores ran low. And when the Cree cut someone off, that usually meant they'd killed 'em.

The Frenchman knew his tenuous time was nearly up. He'd have to do something about that, and soon.

14. COLTER'S HELL

The days continued, though they grew shorter and colder. It was the dead of winter and Colter was in the thick of it. Snow crunched under every step and the wind howled constantly. Food was scarce, for game was hiding or wintering and all that grew had long since ceased. The rivers were of course teaming with fish, most under the frozen ice, but the mountain man had as much of a dislike for them as Captains Lewis and Clark had. Even when they'd been bordering on starvation while crossing the Rockies they hadn't stooped to eating fish, and Colter wasn't about to now. Not that he needed to – his supplies were sound and his health good. It'd been an enjoyable solo trek through the wilderness so far, with amazing sights, wonderful sounds, and one of the greatest senses of tranquility that he'd ever experienced.

Colter had passed by Bighorn Lake a week before, as he'd called it, for it'd come off the Big Horn River, it's towering canyons rising up on either side as the water snaked its way through the mountains there. He kept on the dreaded stink water of the Shoshone River, for that was the only route west. Well, it was the only route west that *he* knew of...so far. After moving overland from the Yellowstone he'd followed the mountains south until he'd met up with the Big Horn. He knew he didn't want to go past it, as that would take him too far east, into the territory that George was to explore. So he'd shot out westward from there, following the Shoshone, and regretting it all the while as he covered his nose, the better to avoid the water's terrible smells.

He continued on, unmolested save for the weather. No Indians at all were around him, it seemed, and he wasn't really surprised – it was the dead of winter, after all. Any smart Indian would be back at his village, in his tepee with the fire blazing, and most likely with a squaw or two to keep him company. Colter smiled at that, thinking of Forest and their trip to the A'anninen the winter before. In the end the man's desire had been the death of him. Still, Colter thought, shaking his head, who could have expected an ambush that day on the river?

The mountain man shook the thoughts away and kept on trekking. He reached Heart Mountain, the name he gave to a solitary peak jutting up out of one low range, one with a slight indentation on the top that resembled a heart. Perhaps it was just that his own heart was feeling lonely, Colter thought as he walked past the mountain for a day or more before turning south. It was a good a spot as any, he figured, and a noticeable one, should he need to come back this way for whatever reason. He doubted he would, however, for this winter expedition was about as dull as they came.

~~~

The dullness continued all along the stinking river, though Colter kept well enough away from it to escape the worst of it, except when the wind picked up from that direction. Other than that, it was much the same as last winter, after he'd gone it alone – walking, thinking, and looking. There wasn't much else you could do in the middle of nowhere and with no one else around. He wasn't much of a talker with other people, and the idea of talking to himself wasn't an appealing one. So the days passed by in silence for the most part, the world going on its merry way despite him.

That all changed one day as he neared the strangest of sights. In the far distance he could see what looked to be campfires, for nothing but smoke could create that. Colter knelt down, looked around, and tightened his grip on his gun. There must be a village around here, he figured, and most likely that would be the Crow. He hoped it was, for he was trying to run into some of them.

The mountain man set out, nearing the smoke but staying in the trees while doing so. He needn't have bothered, he soon realized, for what he was seeing wasn't the smoke from campfires but some kind of smoke belching up right there from the earth. His eyes narrowed and his hand moved up to rub at his jaw. This was unlike anything Colter had seen before, and he was getting a bad feeling about the whole area. It wasn't natural, that was for sure, more like some kind of wasteland on the landscape, the devil's dance hall or some other hell on earth.

He pressed on, his earlier wariness and apprehension turning to curiosity and intrigue. The area was pure wonder. Bubbling pools of water, most clear but quite a few milky or grey, were spread all across the landscape. With care and ease the mountain man walked up to one of the pools, one of the clear ones. It was hot, steam rising up off of it, but he still bent down to see how hot it was.

"Yow!" he yelled, stumbling back to land on his bottom in the snow.

He quickly stuck his finger down in that snow, for he'd burned it something fierce in the scalding water. If a man were to fall into a pool like that he'd be dead in moments. That opinion was confirmed a short time later as the mountain man trudged on, passing by the various pools, for one held the carcass of an elk, a good-sized one too, with six points on each antler. It was big and healthy and Colter could only figure that it'd gotten into a fight with another six-point buck only to come out on the losing end. It was but halfway submerged in the steaming pool after all, just the head and shoulders and mighty antlers. He shook his head as he passed by, for it was quite the waste of a fine creature.

There were no more dead animals in any of the pools that Colter passed by that day, nor the mighty fountains of steam and water that shot up into the air. Those seemed to be clustered in one area, and as he moved evermore south, they faded from view, the same as the pools. By the next day he was out of the hellish area and back to regular-looking land. He was thankful for it too, for that particular spot of wilderness had no earthly right to be there.

15. SKIRTING THE MOUNTAINS

Colter continued moving south, skirting the Absaroka Range. Days passed in the company of the mountains, the towering peaks shooting up on his right side. Jagged teeth was more like it, the mountain man thought, for the mountains had the tendency to shoot up every few hundred yards in a towering pinnacle that stood high over the surrounding range. Those peaks were hundreds of feet above him, maybe thousands, covered with snow and about as forbidding as could be. Colter couldn't imagine having to pass over them, wasn't sure if you could. No, it was skirting beside them, moving south, hoping a break would come, a pass of some sort that would allow travel to the west, and eventually back north on their other side. Colter had decided that he'd make the turn west once he reached that pass, for it'd inevitably turn up. Already the mountain man had gone more than 150 miles south, probably more, and if he hoped to make it back to Manuel and his fort by spring, he'd better be making that turn quick.

Colter was getting anxious about making that turn until he encountered the pass a few days later. It was located between the mountains and another range that continued on south, a set he called the Owl Creek Mountains on account of the small creek he'd stopped at the day before, one that'd had an owl perched nearby. He'd seen another smaller pass the week before and dozens of miles further north, but he'd skipped it. He knew from talks with the Mandan and the Crow that his current route would eventually lead him to the Wind River. That was Crow Indian country, and that's where he'd find the trade that Manuel was so set upon. He'd also find guides, he hoped, men that could show him the best route back north on the other side of the mountains, perhaps saving him a bit of time. Colter wasn't quite sure of the time, but he figured Christmas had passed a week before. More than likely he was in the first or second week of 1808. He scoffed and shook his head at the thought – years and dates and even time didn't much matter out here.

~~~

The three Wise Ones entered the chief's tent at the same moment, just as they'd been bidden to do.

"Sit, have a pipe," Chief He Who Shouts said as soon as they'd entered, gesturing for them to sit down around the fire that took up the middle of the tepee. There were fine bearskin rugs laid all about, and a large peace pipe sitting on one. The Wise Ones did as he said, and were soon passing the pipe back and forth, smoke filling the air around them.

"The reason I've called you here," the chief said in

that slow way of his, looking off into the past or future the way he did, "is because my time is coming to an end."

"No!" the three Wise Ones said at once, but the chief stayed their concerns with his upraised hand. "Please," he said, "you've been waiting for me to die for months, years in some cases." That last was directed at Buffalo Child, who'd been a Wise One the longest. The man wisely kept his tongue.

"Which of us will you choose to take your place?" Silver Heart asked next, after a few moments of silence had passed. It was the tradition among the Piegan Blackfeet, and had been for the past two generations, for the chief to choose his successor from the Wise Ones when he felt it was his time. The first succession had gone off quite well, mainly because there'd only been one Wise One at the time. The next hadn't gone off so smoothly, what with seven Wise Ones, but they'd managed. Going to war with the Nez Perce and the Hidatsa at the same time, and on two fronts, had done much to cut down on any backstabbing that might have come about, mainly because five of the remaining Wise Ones had been killed. One hadn't, and that'd been Buffalo Child's father. He'd died waiting to become chief, and his son had vowed that he'd never suffer the same fate.

"That is for you to decide," He Who Shouts said, eliciting a round of surprised looks from the Wise Ones.

"*Us?*" Stone Bear shouted out. "How are we to decide amongst ourselves?"

"You aren't," the chief said, scoffed was more like it, "you're supposed to go out into the wilderness and let it decide for you."

"The wilderness, but..."

He Who Shouts frowned at Buffalo Child's confusion. "Whichever of you three comes back alive, that's the new chief," he shouted, reminding the men and any close outside why he was named what he was.

"He means we're to go out and find those whites," Silver Heart said, looking at the other two seated beside him, "and perhaps a little betrayal and treachery as well." He looked up to see if he'd been correct in his summation, and seeing the wide smile on the chief's face told him he had.

Buffalo Child smiled, for his Otter Band was the strongest in the tribe, much stronger than Stone Bear's Skunk Band, and certainly stronger than whatever remnants of Silver Heart's offshoot Otter Band remained. If any "treachery," as Silver Heart hinted at, should come about, then Buffalo Child was the most likely to benefit from it...if he wasn't its outright cause.

Beside him, Stone Bear frowned, something that the chief picked up on. "What's the matter?" he asked, looking down at the leader of the Skunk Band. "Didn't you say the other night how you wanted to lead your band out to find the whites? What's the problem?"

"The problem's that the Skunk Band isn't as powerful as it once was, isn't–"

"I didn't say anything about taking your bands with you," the chief said, again with that smile of his.

"No bands, but..."

"I'll give you your sons instead," the chief said as Buffalo Child trailed off, unsure of what to say to this recent development. "I'll give you your sons and their friends. They call themselves the Otter and Skunk Bands enough when they're horsing around, after all. Well, it's time for them to show us what they got!" He laughed. "And that way the playing field is level as well."

Buffalo Child was about to speak up in protest, but He Who Shouts held up his hand and stopped him.

"This is my final word on the matter," he said, giving them all a hard look. "You'll have your wits and your weapons, and you'll also have your sons and their friends. Your warriors stay home." He gave them another hard look. "If you can't lead a group of boys out in the wilderness for a few weeks, how are you going to lead the most powerful tribe on the plains?"

None of the Wise Ones had an answer for that, but each knew the man was right. It was why he was chief, after all, and why he had been for so long.

"Now go," the chief said, "go and make me proud, but more than that, make your sons proud." He gave each a long look at that last pronouncement, just as the men were rising to leave, and gave it to Silver Heart longest of all. It'd been he, after all, that'd lost a son to the whites the previous summer. How that would play into things out in the wild Chief He Who Shouts had no idea, but he made a promise to himself that he'd live long enough to find out.

16. AT THE FORT

The wind howled as it whipped through the lowlands where the two rivers met, both nearly frozen now, so cold was it outside. That didn't stop Manuel Lisa from standing watch over all that he'd created, and all that he considered his own. Calling it his own was a lot easier with the men around him, and the weapons they had. He held one of those weapons now.

The Spaniard preferred his "Brown Bess," and most men on the trapping and trading venture had heard all about it. The musket was British, as most guns carried by serious traders were, and had been made in 1740. The guns had come about during the twelve-year reign of Queen Anne at the beginning of the 18th-century and then their manufacture had continued under the thirteen-year reign of George I. The weapons had a 46-inch barrel with an eleven-gauge bore. Those guns had no bridle nor did they have a pan cover, and unlike many muskets, their lock plate's underside had a noticeable upward curve. Four ramrod pipes were set against the heavy brass mountings and the butt plate's ornamental tang extended far up the comb of the stock. It weighed twelve pounds in all and due to its later manufacture, though had escaped the shortened barrels that subsequent guns suffered from. Those had come about under George II, with steel as opposed to wooden ramrods, and a pan cover. Manuel's musket did have a pan cover, something that had been added later. In that regard it looked much like the "Brown Bess" the soldiers in the Revolution had used, and several of the men had mentioned how they'd seen a few growing up.

Manuel was stroking that Brown Bess now, and staring out over the twelve-foot wall of the fort. Fort Raymond was of about the same type of construction as most of the other types of forts that dotted what many still considered the French-Canadian wilderness. The ground plan was a rectangle, with the side walls coming in at 250 feet. Most forts of that type measured 100 to 400 feet, but owing to the lateness of the season, Manuel had compromised and allowed for the construction of a smaller area. The men had been happy, and the Spaniard too – they'd done a good job and it was clear they'd have the protection they needed, both from the elements and whatever hostile tribes might have already set their sights on them. For protection the fort was enclosed with strong walls of wood, called palisades, which were made of pickets from 12 feet high and 6 inches thick. Again, Manuel had compromised, for he would have preferred 18 feet high and 8 inches thick, like some of the stronger forts dotting the Lower Missouri or like those he'd heard of on the far northern reaches of the Red River where the French fur trapping took place. In some cases the pickets were squared and set close together; in others they were half-round pieces formed by sawing logs in half. The Spaniard had made it clear he didn't care which the men found easiest to make, so long as make them they did. The pickets were set from three feet in the ground and earth was banked up to a small height against them. That was one area Manuel had *not* been willing to compromise on, the depth the wall logs were planted into the ground. He wasn't going to have the fort fall down around him, that was for sure. The fort had musketry loopholes along the top of the wall embankment. For the purpose of guard duty, and also for active defense, a plank walk was bracketed to the inside of the pickets about four feet below the top. This allowed those on guard duty to walk there and observe the ground outside.

The location of the fort had been chosen as much for the spot where the rivers met, its defensive capabilities, but also the nearby timber area. The latter was important not only for constructing the fort but for making mackinaw boats, which were hallowed out cottonwood logs fashioned to the desired proportions. When it came to trapping further afield on some of the smaller offshoots and streams, the boats came in mighty hand.

So the fort was primarily a square blockhouse, the lower part of which would store furs, the upper occupied by the men. Several small out buildings were constructed as well, only large enough for a few supplies, and a few outhouses for when nature called. There was a large garden in the back for spring and another area had been cleared for a watchtower, though the construction of that would have to wait. For defense the men relied on two of those blockhouses, placed at diagonally opposite corners of the fort. They were square in plan, 15 feet on a side, with two stories, and covered with a roof. The lower floor was a few feet above the level of the ground and was loop-holed for small artillery, something which Manuel knew all of the more important frontier posts possessed, even if his did not. Above the artillery floor was another for the musketry defense, with three loop holes on each exposed face. The blockhouse stood entirely outside of the main enclosure, its inner corner joining the corner of the fort so that it flanked two sides; that is, the defenders in each bastion could fire along the outer face of two sides of the fort and thus prevent any attempt to scale or demolish the walls. The fort would prove good for an encampment not only for the men, but surrounding tribes as well. These were Indians that Manuel hoped would come to trade, bringing their furs, and eventually over time, their allegiance to America. Boats could be protected during the winter, hauled out of the water and protected from the winter elements. The drinking water would also be sought, for the Yellowstone ran much clearer than the Bighorn, which was cloudy with mud.

Life at the fort was turning into a steady routine. It hadn't taken long for some of the neighboring tribes to figure out they were there, either. The Crow had been the first to come, followed by some members of the A'anninen tribe and then even some Hidatsa. So the men spent their days receiving and dismissing bands of Indians who came in to trade, for the most part, and built the fort the rest of the time. Those with no carpentry experience watched the country for signs of buffalo, and when they came, sent hunting parties out for meat. Others spent their time cutting wood for the continual fires that needed to burn. And of course there was keeping the accounts, journals and correspondence of the fort, something that fell to Manuel and those closest to him. Everyone took part in baling and pressing furs for St. Louis.

The fort came along nicely as December had changed into January. It was built with spruce and fir and pine mainly, with tar and pitch used for support and quite a bit of cottonwood and cedar thrown in as well. Really, whatever the men could find that was checked-off on by the carpenters. There were twelve of them, men that were primarily brought because of their abilities there. Come the rest of the year they'd be put to other uses, and when the trappers and hunters went out, they'd stay behind, doing the more menial tasks that needed to be done when upwards of fifty men were living together in a confined space. No women were with them, so sewing, cleaning, cooking, laundry, and all else fell to the men.

So far there'd been no attacks, and now that it was already into the heaviest of winter, Manuel doubted there would be. Still, he stood watch most days, stroking that gun of his, looking out and expecting there to be.

The problem, as the Spaniard saw it, was that the Indians were riled up. Something had gotten them excited, the Blackfeet in particular. He looked over at the tall walls and parapets and was once again thankful he'd been adamant they be built so high. Sour looks were all the Blackfeet directed toward them, which was a lot better than angry arrows. The Assiniboine had been the same, coming within sight of the fort, but not within gunshot range. They'd been startled by the swivel gun on the river coming up, and Manuel hoped they stayed that way. He knew they wouldn't forever, and likely over winter, as tales from the various tribes spread, they'd overcome their fear. After all, they had the numbers, and with a few dozen losses, maybe more, they could overpower whatever resistance the whites gave, however much the men had managed to entrench themselves.

Manuel frowned and let out a sigh. There was still the chance the Blackfeet and the Assiniboine could ally together, or perhaps even some of the Sioux. The Spaniard knew if that happened they'd be done, overrun before they even knew what hit 'em.

The sound of the gate creaking shut for the night drew his attention. The winter wind howled and the snow gusted up before his eyes. He stared out into the encroaching blackness and thought of George, the half-Shawnee half-French-Canadian scout. He was to the east, in the lands they knew were relatively safe, relatively friendly. It was Colter that the Spaniard worried about. He'd gone to the south and to the west, into lands held by the Crow, but also frequented by the Blackfeet. Captains Lewis and Clark had had a run in with the Indians, and Manuel wondered if some of the hatred that surely existed amongst the Blackfeet for the whites would transfer to the mountain man. There was little he could do now, he knew, but hope, hope that the man made it back come spring.

17. THE WIND RIVER

Colter kept up his pace, one that was steady and anything but slow. He figured he was putting in a good ten miles a day, a little more when the ground was flat and there were no rivers in the way. There wasn't much of the latter, for Colter had passed over the Wind River earlier that day. He'd walked its banks for a good mile, looking for a shallow-enough spot to wade across, one with quite a few rocks so he wouldn't get too wet. It'd taken awhile, but he'd found it, and was now skirting the southern reaches of the Absaroka Range. The mountains were brown and drab and just one continuous row of even rock towering thousands of feet above him. Occasionally there'd be a single peak jutting out, a lone tooth in a scraggly-toothed mouth, and Colter took note of them, should he need to come back this way.

That wasn't the plan, of course. Colter was doing a complete circuit now, he knew, one that would take him down and around and then back up, all the way around several mountain ranges, or more aptly, through their passes so he didn't have to trudge over them, which would have been impossible.

Following the Absarokas Colter made it to the Wind River Range. The mountains there were stark and gray and pointing upward at the heavens like row upon row of jagged and mismatched teeth. Snow dotted their upper reaches, even this early in the season...or late, depending on how you wanted to look at it. Colter knew all the names of the mountains for he'd been briefed on such the night before leaving the fort, as well as that morning. They knew what the names were for the men had spoken with members of the surrounding tribes, even if that information was often imparted third-hand, or from the Mandans hundreds of miles away. And it wasn't hard for Colter to know when one range changed into another, as happened a couple days later when the stark grayness of the Wind River Range gave way to the pinkish-white of the Gros Ventre Mountains. Colter knew they didn't have that color, but the way the early morning and late afternoon sun hit them, and it sure looked like God had bent down with his paintbrush, fancifully working the canvas of reality for all those lucky enough to see.

Some that saw those mountains often were the Crow, and Colter knew he was smack dab in the middle of their territory. He had to find them, he knew, for Manuel back at the fort was depending on him to do so. The fur trapper and businessman had been adamant that trade with the Indians be opened up. It was something that needed to be done, but this year it was a must – their late arrival to the Yellowstone meant that the rest of 1807 had been cutoff to them. Any trapping that was to take place on this venture would have to take place in spring, the few months the men had before the first shipments were sent downriver to St. Louis. Trade was therefore critical, for it meant they could build up the same level of furs but without all the work. The Indians in the region had known for years that trapping beaver, skinning them, and securing the furs was a lucrative way for them to take advantage of the westward expansion of the whites. The Crow knew that especially well, and the mountain man expected that there were bundles of furs just waiting at some far flung villages, villages which *he* was supposed to find. He hadn't had much luck with that so far, and that's why he doubled back upon reaching the Gros Ventre Mountains. The Crow would be around the Wind River or around the Green, and Colter meant to stay in that general vicinity until he ran into them...even if it took all winter.

Thankfully, however, it didn't.

Just a few days after turning back the mountain man was moving up the eastern bank of the Wind River when something caught his ear. Colter came to a halt, looked sideways, and tried to make his ears hear for all they were worth. Something had made a sound...something. It wasn't the wind rustling the pine needles or snow falling from leaves. It wasn't a winter bird pecking away nor was it the endless sound of his own boots crunching through the icy snow. The mountain man had heard something, however, and stood there just within the tree line, the vast plain that rose up to meet the Absaroka Mountains stretching out before him just as empty as ever. The wind blew, swirling flakes about, biting at his ears and nose and fingertips. Colter eased one of those fingertips onto the trigger of his rifle, brought the gun up to his shoulder. Something was out there, Colter knew that for sure. That's when he heard the crunching of the snow.

Colter spun about, bringing his rifle up to his face, but then a moment later he lowered it. The Indian he was suddenly face to face with smiled as he did so.

"Hello," he said in English.

"Hello," Colter replied, and then in his limited Crow said, "I've been looking for you."

The Crow Indian's smile grew larger at that, and he put up his arm, motioning for something. A moment later Colter saw two more braves materialize from the trees, each no more than ten feet away from the other, but just as hidden if they'd been miles away.

"Two days," the lead Crow said in heavily accented English, "two days we track you."

Colter nodded. It was clear that this was the Crow band's leader, and his English wasn't that good. It was a sight better than Colter's Crow, however. He'd never been much good with the Siouan languages of the plains tribes, had always had a better ear for the Dhegiha languages of the tribes closer to the Mississippi, but that didn't do him much good now.

"You speak English," he said, then a moment later, "*comment est votre français?*"

The Crow shook his head. "You think my English bad, wait to you hear my French!" The brave spoke a few quick words in Crow to his companions, and a moment later the three were chuckling. When that died down the Indian put his hands to his mouth and whistled. A few moments later Colter could hear more crunching in the snow, and then there were four more Crow Indians in their midst. Colter shook his head and smiled, and the Crow did the same.

"You whites," the brave said with a smile, "always so surprised to hear what quiet sounds like."

The mountain man smiled again, and soon he was moving along with the band, westward past the Wind River and further into unknown lands.

18. ON THE HUNT

Buffalo Child clicked his tongue and his horse moved forward, into the Shoshone River and then slowly across. The other mounted Blackfeet did the same, and then those that were on foot, which was most. Wolf Calf looked back at those that were walking and once again thanked his lucky stars that he'd been given a horse. As if reading his mind, his father Stone Bear glanced back, caught his eye, and gave a slight nod. Wolf Calf smiled inwardly – he really was a brave now.

My, how far he'd come in just the past few months. Late last year before winter had set in he'd been in this same area, though alone and without permission. He'd come down the Bighorn River, hoping to enter into another vision quest, but it wasn't meant to be. In the end he'd been gone from the village for six days, and when he'd come back he'd been chided something fierce. A lot of that had come about because the vision quest Wolf Calf had been seeking had never occurred.

He sighed when he thought back on those days many months before, and also what had happened. For it'd been on that river that Wolf Calf had come across the two Crow, boys like himself, both also away from their tribe without permission. They'd been brothers, and they'd spotted the young Blackfoot first. Wolf Calf had tensed up, bringing up his bow and arrow, but the boys had only laughed. Wolf Calf had picked up a bit of Crow, but not as much as the others had picked up of his own language. They spoke up, using his tribe's own words to sooth and calm him. It'd worked, and before he'd really known what'd happened, Wolf Calf was walking with them, talking, and soon enough, laughing.

The boys spent three days together, splitting off of the Big Horn to head west on the Shoshone. From there they'd headed overland to yet another river, the Clarks Fork, or Small Fork as they knew it as. That's when things had gone wrong, oh so terribly wrong. Wolf Calf looked up at the big, blue sky and shuddered despite himself. *What had they seen that night?*

He shook the thoughts from his head, not wanting to relive that night or what'd occurred. He looked around. They were fourteen strong – the three Wise Ones in the lead, their three sons, and then the leading young braves of the Otter and Skunk Bands, five young braves like Wolf Calf and then three older braves, men that each of the Wise Ones trusted and had been allowed to bring along. Chief He Who Shouts had been adamant, Wolf Calf later learned, that the Wise Ones only go out with young braves and one trusted friend. He was really testing the men, really ensuring that the Piegan Blackfeet would be led by the most competent amongst them. Wolf Calf wondered if his father would be the one that succeeded in the end. He knew that if his father didn't then his own standing in the tribe would be finished. It'd be better to be dead.

Wolf Calf shook the thought away and looked out past the river. It was the Shoshone, and crossing south of it meant they were truly in Crow lands. Would they run into the Indians, perhaps even come to blows with them? It was likely, the young brave knew, for Silver Heart had made it clear that the white was travelling with a small band of the Indians, one he'd met up with just a day or two before. Silver Heart was the best tracker in the tribe, and spent most of his time walking, following the trail that was so easy. They were a few days behind, but since the white and the Crow were on foot, it'd be very soon now.

Wolf Calf smiled. He was ready for vengeance, ready to redeem himself, ready to take his rightful place in the tribe.

19. CROSSING PATHS

Colter was enjoying his time with the Crow. There was only one that spoke any English, Toop was his name, and Colter was learning quite a bit about the area from him. It was a slow process, what with the language barrier due to Toop's lack of skill, though Colter was always quick to point out that his language skills were nothing to brag about. Already the Crow were urging Colter to come back to their village near the Snake River, and the mountain man had finally agreed. They were moving westward now, hoping to come to the last of the Wind River Range that very day. Another couple days would have Colter back at the Gros Ventre Mountains and then he knew it wouldn't be long before the Snake was sighted.

The day began to grow dark just as the mountains

they'd been following for the past two days began to recede and grow smaller.

"We'll make camp soon," Toop said, motioning ahead toward a thick copse of trees that was near the base of the Absarokas.

Colter nodded and they pressed on. They were walking in the tree line, the better to be off the main plain. Toop had been adamant that this area was safe for them now, but still, he wasn't going to walk right out in the open. No, it was better to walk in the tree line, a few dozen feet from the open plains that stretched for dozens of miles before the distant mountains gobbled them up again. They were walking in those trees and looking forward to settling down for the night when up ahead Cottay came to a stop. He was the tracker for the band, and typically walked a good fifty yards ahead of the others. Never before had Colter seen him come to a stop so suddenly, and the mountain man tensed up. A quick look around showed him that the other eight members of the band had done the same.

Colter narrowed his eyes and looked at Toop. The Crow brave was smiling and shaking his head, those bright white teeth of his a stark contrast against that darker face. It was clear he thought no threat existed. The sight put the mountain man at ease, and he relaxed. Any moment now he expected Toop to shout back at him to take it easy – let them handle it. This was Crow country, after all, and Colter should know enough to let them lead.

That shout didn't come, however, for in the midst of that smile there was the most unusual thing – a stone flew out and hit Toop right on the side of the head. The smile faltered as surprise registered in the man's brain. That seemed to be all that registered, however, for a moment later Toop began to fall over, that smile still somewhat on his face, though it was gone by the time he hit the ground. He lay there, unmoving, and that's when the arrows flew out.

"Down!" Colter heard one of the Crow shout out in his native tongue, but it was too late – at least a dozen arrows flew out at them, and the brave that'd uttered the warning only got one through his leg for his effort.

Colter grabbed hold of his gun and looked toward the trees, northward to where the attack was coming from. There was a musket shot nearby, and he knew one of the Crow had gotten a shot off. Another shot came, and he felt confident this attack could be repulsed. No shots were coming from the trees, just arrows. That's when Colter saw movement and brought the musket up to his face, readying for a shot, just waiting to take aim...

"Ah!" Colter shouted, and he jerked his head away from the gun to look down. There was an arrow through his right leg, just above the knee. Grimacing, he bent down and put the butt of his gun on the ground, brought his hands back up, gripped the arrow and then broke the haft off.

"Ah!" came the sound from his lips, though more of a grunt this time. He grabbed his gun and that's when he looked around for the first time. All around him, Crow braves were down, including Cottay far ahead. Worse, however, was that those not hit were slinking off, running instead of fighting. The mountain man gritted his teeth and bit his lip, the better not to cry out at them, calling them dogs and betrayers and whatever else he could. It might make him feel good, but it'd only draw the attention of the band of Indians attacking them, Blackfeet most likely, if Colter had to guess. The good news was that the arrows from the trees were following the retreating Indians, and not focused on him. The mountain man got some satisfaction out of that, and instead of returning fire, he got up and turned about, deciding it'd be best to head the other way, getting out of the fight entirely.

He did just that, and ran right into an Indian brave.

The smile the young man gave him made it clear – this was not a friend.

~~~

Arapoosh heard the gunshot, then another one close behind it. He craned his neck and put his hand to his ear, listening. A few whoops and shouts came to him. *Blackfeet*, he thought, for he'd seen their horse's tracks and even spotted one the day before from a hilltop. They'd spotted something it seemed, and boy did it have them excited!

Without wasting another second, the young River Crow was on his feet and moving west.

~~~

The brave smiled a bit wider then started to move forward, his tomahawk beginning to go up. Colter frowned, and did the only thing he could. He brought up the Northwest Trade Gun and fired. The advancing brave was so close that the force of the blast in his chest sent him flying backward a good five or six feet to crumple against a tree, dead.

The mountain man didn't waste a second – he dashed forward past the Indian, leaning down to grab the tomahawk. Colter never knew when–

THUNK!

The mountain man's eyes went wide at the axe that'd embedded itself into the tree trunk just inches from his face. The weapon would have taken him right in the head had he not bent down. He then looked over to see an angry-looking brave just inches from him, and desperately trying to wedge the thing free. It was stuck, Colter knew, and he didn't hesitate. He brought up the tomahawk he'd just grabbed and slammed it down into the brave's chest, right between the arms that were outstretched and struggling to free the weapon. Blood spurted out, right into Colter's face and beard. He let go and saw the brave's body begin to fall backward. By the time it hit the ground the mountain man was running as best he could, the arrow wound in his leg bleeding something fierce.

~~~

Slow Breeze saw the white man dash off, or at least try to. He was stumbling and hobbling more than anything, and the Blackfoot brave smiled. The arrow he'd put through the man's leg would be more than enough for him to track him, catch him, and kill him. He didn't have the yellow hair, but the hair was certainly *yellowish*, the most Slow Breeze had ever seen at least. This *must* be the man Wolf Calf had seen.

He gave a quick look around at his companions, the other Blackfeet Indians fighting alongside Buffalo Child, the Wise One he gave allegiance to. All were preoccupied, most with killing Crow. As far as Slow Breeze could tell, he was the only one that'd seen the white. He scoffed and shook his head and stood up. Arrows were still flying about, but they were going in the wrong direction – east toward where the Crow were fleeing. They should have been heading west, and that's what Slow Breeze began to do, move west, his bow in his hand, his tomahawk in the other, and a wicked smile on his face.

20. A CHANCE ENCOUNTER

Arapoosh dashed through the underbrush, not caring how much sound he made. There was an attack going on nearby, and he meant to find out what it was. He meant to find out...

The young Crow brave came to a stop, his eyes going wide. Something was crashing right through the bushes toward him, something loud and–

CRASH!

Colter tore through the bushes, not caring at all how much sound he made for he'd managed to reload his rifle. There was more than enough sound behind him as it was, the sound of whooping and hollering and people dying. He'd had enough of that, and with his wounded leg he...

The mountain man came to a halt, his feet struggling for purchase on the stick-strewn and pebbly ground that was beneath the thin layer of snow, for there before him was a young Indian boy, a spear held up over his arm in a ready-to-throw gesture.

Arapoosh didn't know what to make of it, for he'd never seen a man like this before, at least not out in the wilds. He was a white, that much was clear, but one with a flowing beard covered in blood, scrubby clothing, and quite the large rifle or musket in his hands. He also had a savage wound in his leg, for the young brave could clearly see the blood-soaked trousers and right moccasin that'd turned red.

The two stared at one another for a moment, the eyes of each narrowing in surprise, concern, and question. Was this friend or foe before them, each wondered, and neither could tell. Those thoughts were disrupted a moment later, for the sound of more crashing through the bushes could clearly be heard.

Colter decided that the boy in front of him wasn't as dangerous as what was likely following him, a Blackfoot brave that wouldn't hesitate as the boy had. He turned about and brought up his rifle, thinking back on the winter before when he'd been staring into some bushes, a pursuer coming at him unseen, and he just sitting and waiting for the moment to pull the trigger. He wasn't disappointed.

Just then Slow Breeze tore through the bushes, expecting to see nothing more than another set of bushes that needed to be torn through. The white was ahead of him he knew, but not for one second had the Blackfoot expected the man to be right there, *and* pointing his gun his way. Slow Breeze closed his eyes up tight as his rush continued, fully expecting the bullet to tear into him.

Colter saw the brave rush out of the bushes and he didn't hesitate. His finger pulled back on the trigger and the Northwest Trade gun's hammer slammed down onto the pan...and misfired. A blinding cloud of white smoke rose up and hit Colter right in the face, and together with the kick from the rifle, he was thrown backward. Ahead of him, Slow Breeze smiled.

Arapoosh couldn't believe what he was seeing. First a white, then a Blackfoot, and then a gun that did more harm to the man that'd fired it! The white was down on the ground now and the Blackfoot was rushing up, bloodlust in his eyes, a smile on his face, and his tomahawk raised high for the killing blow. Arapoosh didn't hesitate.

The spear flew from the young Crow's hand as he hurled his arm forward and then released. Slow Breeze was too intent upon his killing dive to see the projectile heading his way, a sharpened cottonwood limb nearly four feet in length. The point of it plunged into the Blackfoot brave's chest and pushed him backward slightly so that his killing jump was blocked. A look of surprise came over his face as he fell to the ground to land on his bottom, and that's when he saw Arapoosh standing there, a firm look of justice on his face. The River Crow were no friends of the Blackfeet, after all, for the hostile tribe had raided them enough times for that to be abundantly clear. All Slow Breeze managed was to drool a bit of blood out of the side of his mouth before his eyes glazed over and he fell on his side, dead, the young brave's spear sticking clean through him.

Colter couldn't believe what he'd just seen, for he'd not viewed the boy as a threat at all. Obviously he was, however, and the mountain man began to reach for the knife at his belt. He did so slowly, however, for he didn't think the boy meant him any harm. That suspicion was confirmed a moment later when the boy shook his head at Colter, then flicked his chin over his shoulder, gesturing for the mountain man to follow him. Colter gave a quick glance back at the dead Blackfoot and then the direction they'd both come from. There could be more, and likely would be when this one didn't come back. Colter looked back at the young brave, nodded, and was soon on his feet and following close behind.

PART III – TRACKING

21. FINDING TRAILS

Wolf Calf tore his tomahawk from the back of the Crow, then spit on the body for good measure. The dogs should have known better than to befriend a white, they should have known.

He straightened up from the dead Crow and then looked around. The members of the Blackfeet band were all doing about the same as him – wiping the blood from their weapons and looking around. In most faces Wolf Calf saw frustration, even anger. The Crow band had only been ten-strong, and the bloodlust of the Blackfeet had only been whetted, not satisfied.

Up ahead Silver Heart stopped, knelt down to the ground, and then put his hand up. Behind him the other two Wise Ones brought their horses to a stop, the only two they had left. The Crow, while retreating, had hit quite a few of the animals, and from the whinnying a short distance away, Wolf Calf knew that some would have to be put down. Like the white, they'd all soon be on foot.

Wolf Calf looked over at Little Mouse and Dog Hair and they did the same, the braves walking further behind them then doing the same as well so that all fourteen of them were stopped, or at least all that were present. Wolf Calf saw that two of them were still gone. After a moment Buffalo Child and Stone Bear moved up and the men were soon discussing something, likely tracks and the direction the white had gone, Wolf Calf knew.

They were still following the Shoshone River and had been for the past several days. Heart Mountain had appeared just the day before, signaling to them that the Snowy Range was coming up to their north, the Absaroka Range to their south. Between the two mountain ranges was a single pass, the Blackfeet and all other area tribes knew, one that started at the hellish landscape they all called "Other World." The area was awash in bubbling cauldrons, hot pools, and other hazards that could take an unsuspecting brave quickly. Wolf Calf had grown up listening to tales around the fire about strong braves heading into the area, either on vision quests or hunting treks, with all invariably meeting their end there in some gruesome and hellish fashion. The hell holes didn't take up the whole area, however, and there was a skinny mountain pass that'd take travelers to the large lake that dominated that side of the mountain, called Yellowstone Lake. The Blackfeet had begun calling "Other World" Yellowstone because of the French, who'd named it after the yellow rocks that appeared in the river, especially near the towering falls further to the west. It wasn't yellow rocks that the three Wise Ones were arguing over, however, and after glancing at Little Mouse and Dog Hair and getting the nod, the three braves moved forward to get a better listen, the others behind them doing the same.

"One man?" Stone Bear was saying when they got within earshot. "What is one man going to do for the tribe?"

Buffalo Child gave Stone Bear a hard look. The two men locked gazes for some time, and it was clear to Silver Heart and the braves looking on that relations in the group were already beginning to break down. The dead horses probably had something to do with that, and the frustration it brought.

"That one man killed Silver Heart's son," Buffalo Child the leader of the Otter Band said, raising his tomahawk up to point at the other Wise One, "and another young brave lost his life as well." He scoffed. "You ask what one man is going to do for the tribe? It'll bring justice, that's what it'll do, it'll bring a sense of peace to the mothers of those braves, and their fathers as well."

"I've never known death following death to bring about peace," Silver Heart said, and Stone Bear saw the vehement look in Buffalo Child's face give way to a frown. The wise one lowered his tomahawk, looked over at Silver Heart, and shook his head. "You've never known a lot of things, and that's why no one's ever seriously considered you as chief."

Silver Heart was a bit taken aback by that comment, Stone Bear saw, but Buffalo Child paid it no heed as his attention was back on who he considered his true rival for leadership of the Piegan Blackfoot tribe, Stone Bear.

Wolf Calf looked from his father to Buffalo Child and back again, unsure of what he should do. *Could it come to blows?* he thought, but then shook the thought away – it would never come to that...would it?

"These whites that infest our lands are nothing more than a nuisance, a vermin that we can sweep aside," Buffalo Child continued, "and sweep them aside we will. There are more important things for us to do, such as pushing the Shoshone and Nez Perce from our lands, and then the Crow further south. Never mind that they say they were here first – they're our true enemies! They hold the riches we'll need in order to defeat the whites and take their trade goods, the better to trade with the whites up north, the French and British."

"And what riches are those?" Stone Bear said, his face much like his name, a mask of stone and unreadable.

"Horses," Buffalo Child said with a smile, "horses. The same beasts your son tried to take from the whites, and nearly succeeded at. *He's* smart enough to see how things are...unlike his father."

Stone Bear shook his head. "You're wrong, Buffalo Child, for it's not the horses of our neighboring tribes we should be concerned with, but the ever increasing number of whites that are showing up in our lands. It used to be a few men, often alone and in need of our help. More and more, however, it's groups of men, and with an attitude of conquest as opposed to cooperation. The whites are our true enemies, and we should ally ourselves with the neighboring tribes in a bid to defeat them."

Buffalo Child threw back his head and laughed, a deep and hearty laugh that was more show than anything. At least that's what Silver Heart thought of it as he looked from the Buffalo Child to Stone Bear, who still had that unreadable expression on his face. Silver Heart had never liked the Shoshone or Nez Perce, and he hated the Crow, but Buffalo Child was right – the whites *were* coming more and more, and unlike the tribes, they didn't fight amongst themselves. Even when their language and customs differed, they didn't fight amongst themselves.

"We should go back," Stone Bear said suddenly, something that brought Buffalo Child's laugh to an abrupt end, much to the man's chagrin. He sent a scowl Stone Bear's way, but the Wise One was not dissuaded. "We should go back," he said again, "back to our village, back to Chief He Who Shouts so we can explain to him the real threat that faces us, the force of whites that are setting up right on a river to the east of our lands."

Buffalo Child sneered and looked over at Silver Heart. "This woman has no taste for blood, has no desire to see your son avenged. What do you say to that?"

Silver Heart looked from Buffalo Child to Stone Bear and back again, and thought for several moments before speaking. "I think our fellow Wise One makes sense, and that we should listen to him...but not now. While it's true that the whites gathered on the river are a sizeable force, it was also clear on our passage that they desired peace, and trade. We were met with waves and smiles, even from afar I could see that."

"That's a far cry from the knife in the heart and bullet in the belly that the yellow-capped white gave your son and Sidehill Calf!" Buffalo Child said, and Silver Heart had no choice but to nod to the truth of that. He was about to do more but he and everyone else's attention was diverted to the bushes. They were rustling and everyone tensed up. A moment later a call came out in their native tongue and a few seconds later Strong Foot appeared. He looked at them all, then settled his eyes on Buffalo Child and shook his head. A moment later he brought Slow Breeze's tomahawk around from his back, holding it up for all to see. No one had to say anything to know that Buffalo Child's companion was dead.

"Two sets of tracks," Strong Foot said a moment

later, after the sight had sunk in, "two sets heading west. One is the white, the other is...a boy, or at least a very young brave, not much older than these braves we have with us," he said, gesturing to Wolf Calf and the others.

Buffalo Child nodded after a few moments, looking at them all, then let out a deep sigh. His earlier words now had much more resonance, that was clear to all. A few moments later Silver Heart began to nod, then addressed them.

"Let us go on, after this lone white that brought our tribe so much pain, let us go on," the Wise One said. He then looked at Buffalo Child. "But if circumstances change, know that I might be more favorably inclined to Stone Bear's way of seeing things than yours."

He gave Buffalo Child a hard look with that last declaration, and the braves of the two bands looked at their elders and wondered what would happen next, wondered if the blows they fully expected between Buffalo Child and Stone Bear were finally going to occur.

They didn't, for the leading Wise One nodded and said not a word, just turned and started off again, sticking to the Shoshone River, continuing westward toward the mountain pass...and the white that was heading toward it.

22. THE CREE

Larocque frowned and once again did his best to wrap the mediocre elk skin coat around himself. His prized buffalo robe had been taken by the Cree when he'd been captured after all. To add insult to injury, it'd been traded to the Assiniboine as the first of the winter snows had appeared. Now the Frenchman was freezing most days, and he didn't even have the consoling thought that he could kill his captors and get the robe back – it was gone. There were other buffalo robes, however, and Larocque stared at a couple of them with envy at just that moment. One was worn by Thin Leg, the leader of the band. He didn't take any guff from his subordinates, Larocque knew, and had already killed one member of the band that'd tried to challenge him. They were out too long the Frenchman knew, and Broken Arm had known it too. That brave had come up with some flimsy excuse to go back to the village. That'd been four days ago now, and since then Little Leg had become much more emboldened. Broken Arm was related to one of the main chiefs of their particular Cree tribe, and with him gone, Little Leg's ego had taken hold. Sand Face hadn't helped matters, for the herbalist and medicine-man-in-training was the quintessential 'yes-man' for whoever was in charge. Little Pine wasn't much different, for he just wanted to hunt and kill whites and whatever other tribe they happened to be at war with at the moment. That just left Cut Nose, the band's tracker and one that was beginning to question Thin Leg's leadership just as much as Broken Arm had.

Larocque knew it all, had put it all together from snippets here and little bits there. He wasn't proficient in the Naskapi language but he did know his Algonquin languages, and what these Cree were speaking traced from that. After he'd picked out key words, it'd been easy, what with all the time he'd had. Now he planned to use what he'd learned against his captors...at the first chance he got, that is. Now wasn't it.

The Cree had risen to power along with the rise of the fur trade. As the Hudson's Bay Company moved further inland and further to the West, the Cree found a niche ferrying furs from one trade post to another. They'd also become quite the dealers in pemmican, the dried buffalo meat the trappers relied on so much for sustenance. As the British and the French continued to expand, the Cree were the go-to tribe when anything was needed in the subarctic. The Cree had been a woodlands tribe but had adopted the ways of the plains Indians. They became the Plains Cree, the most westward of the bunch. Fighting the Kootenai and the Snakes to the base of the Rocky Mountains, the Cree became as dominant and warlike as the Blackfeet. Soon the Cree were allied with that tribe, as well as with the Mandan further to the south. Then the sickness came, the smallpox epidemics of 1780 to 1781 that had decimated the western plains tribes, reducing their numbers drastically. Political shakeups occurred as chiefs and elders died and new, younger minds came to the fore. These new leaders of the Cree turned their backs on the Mandans, the tribe that had first given them horses around 1790, and began to take up with the Assiniboine. This led to an alliance with the Chippewa as well, and the Mandan began to be looked down upon.

Larocque remembered one story of a Cree trader buying a musket from the Hudson's Bay Company for fourteen beaver pelts, only to turn around and sell it to a Blackfoot brave for fifty beaver pelts. That was the Cree tribe – about as self-serving as you could get. The trade with the Mandan deteriorated as the Iron Confederacy grew in strength, and that proved disastrous for the Cree as they'd relied on the Mandan for their horses. New sources were sought, mainly with the Arapaho far to the south, where the Spanish used to roam. The A'anninen didn't much like that, and did their best to block the southward path of the tribe. The Confederacy was stopped, though this caused problems with the Blackfeet, who up until that time had been allied with the A'anninen. Their southward trade routes cutoff, the Cree turned west, to the Flathead across the Rockies. That was another tribe the Blackfeet had historically fought against, but the Cree would hear none of it – they needed horses. To the Blackfeet, the best horsemen on the plains and a tribe that never wanted for the beasts, largely because they rarely traded them, this was seen as the final straw. Relations between the Blackfeet and the Cree broke down irreparably, and had been that way for the past few years.

Larocque knew what few to the east knew – the Iron Confederacy of the Blackfeet, Cree and Assiniboine was no more. The Chippewa were taking the place of the Blackfeet, and together the three newly-allied tribes were beginning to wage war on their former friends. That was the environment Larocque had been in for the past several months, and his only hope was that he could use that feud, and the inner-turmoil of this particular band, to somehow stage his escape.

23. A NEW FRIEND

"Alright...slow down," Colter said. They were the first words he'd said to the boy since they'd met up more than an hour before.

They'd hustled out of the area, each running as much as they could on the rocky and uneven ground. For some time now though it was clear that their pursuers had slackened off, somewhat at least, and enough for Colter to figure out who his new companion was. To his surprise, the boy turned at his words, though the mountain man wasn't sure if he'd been understood.

"What are you doing out here?" Arapoosh asked, and Colter was startled to hear him speak English, though it was broken and a bit hard to understand. The young Crow brave could see this, and said, "I know your language from the British trappers that have come through our area."

Colter nodded. "That'd explain it then. What's your name?"

"Arapoosh," the brave said. "What's yours?"

"Colter, John Colter."

The two nodded and sized one another up. Colter put the boy at twelve years old, maybe thirteen. He was young, that was for sure, short for his age too, but his face seemed to hold wisdom beyond his years...or maybe just tiredness. To Arapoosh, the mountain man looked like something that'd crawled in from the wilderness to die. He was unkempt, unwashed, and unshaved. He smelled bad, too, like beaver and raw meat and...Arapoosh didn't want to think about it.

"Thanks for saving me back there," Colter said after a few moments had passed.

"What are you doing here?" Arapoosh asked again. "And what are you going to do about that leg?"

Colter winced at that. He'd had his hands over the wound as much as he could after they'd first started running, and then after a bit he'd pulled out a length of cloth and tied it off. The arrow hadn't gone deep due to the extra furs he'd been wearing to keep out the cold, but it still hurt something fierce. At least the blood flow had been stopped, somewhat, for their continual running sent a jolt of agony through him with each step, as well as a bit of blood from the wound. The cloth was soaked now.

"I'm trying to open up trade with the Crow," Colter said as he looked around and, finding a good-sized rock, sat down. "And as to this leg, I'll have it fixed up as best I can, if you stand watch that is." He flicked his head toward the direction they'd come from, and Arapoosh nodded.

They fell into silence as Colter dug into his bag for a

needle and thread. He'd already pulled the arrow out so now it was just sewing up the wound. The mountain man was good at sewing, as were all the men of the expedition that headed out with the Captains, for there were no women to mend their garments. Sometimes they mended skin too, and when needle and thread weren't handy the right thorn and a long hair would do the trick. Colter was thankful he still had his pack, and after several minutes had gone by, he had the wound stitched up.

"Here," Arapoosh said when he'd finished. He had a poultice of some sort, and the mountain man took it from his hand and smeared it on. "That'll heal it a few days faster, and we'll need them if the Blackfeet are still following us."

"So it's 'we' now, is it?" Colter said as he started putting away his things.

"If you don't mind," Arapoosh said. "When that band of Blackfeet attacked they were on horses, but I saw many of the animals hit by the Crow you were with."

"You're Crow too, aren't you?" Colter asked, and when Arapoosh nodded, he said, "why didn't you go with them?" He narrowed his eyes. "What are *you* doing out here?"

The young brave sighed, then told his story, including the night Thrown in the Spring went missing. He told of the Blackfoot brave he'd encountered, one by the name of Wolf Calf, as well as the ultimate fate of his brother.

"*Sky People?* Colter said when the tale was done. "Who are they?"

"They live in Above World," Arapoosh said, and the look on his face left no doubt in the mountain man's mind that the young brave believed the story. "He was taken one night last winter, and I'm looking for him. Since I'm such a lowly figure in my village, little more than a captive, no one will miss me."

"And what will you do if you find him?" Colter

asked.

Arapoosh didn't know what to say to that, and it was obvious to the mountain man that the boy hadn't thought that far ahead.

"Maybe..." Arapoosh started, "maybe we'll go west, past the mountains, and to new lands with new tribes."

Colter couldn't argue with that. The area around here was anything but welcoming, he'd learned that firsthand twice now. If the young Crow brave wanted to travel with him, then so be it – the mountain man could do with the other set of eyes, *and* that deadly throwing arm.

The two started out a short time after that, and were soon moving north.

24. ESCAPE

The band had stopped on the edge of the river, the Green, Larocque was quite certain. It was midday and time to eat, which for the Frenchman meant whatever scraps were thrown to him.

The Cree were led by their okimahkan, or war chief. He was different from their peace chief, who was more of a diplomat than a warrior. But these were desperate times, what with the Blackfeet totally in control of the area stretching from the North Saskatchewan River down to the upper reaches of the Missouri. Their range also extended westward 300 miles from the Rockies, the area they'd forcibly taken from the Shoshone tribe, who'd fled southward.

That meant the Cree had to be vigilant. With their newfound war with the Blackfeet, they had to be on their guard, too. The Blackfeet were the most militarized and the most violent tribe on the plains, known for their scalping, stealing, and slaves. It was far different from the largely peaceful Cree tribe. In fact, many of the Cree bands hadn't wanted war with the Blackfeet, no matter how powerful their confederacy with the Chippewa and Assiniboine was. They knew the power of the Blackfeet, and the tribe's tendency to keep a grudge. The allied bands had decided in council, however, that war was the only course. That's why they had their war chief, Thin Leg, and he rose up at that moment to address the other four braves. As usual, Larocque listened despite not wanting to, and not for the first time did he kick himself for learning their language.

"We near the end of the Green River," he said, looking at each of his braves in turn, "and that means our path will grow perilous. We're entering the area of the Blackfeet and the Crow." There were a few snickers to that last, but Thin Leg pressed on. "We'll move through the area swiftly, pushing north along the mountains until we get to the bubbling pools. At that point we'll cut east to the opposite range, then move up the Yellowstone and back home."

The braves nodded to their chief's words as they ate their midday meal. All knew that it was the safest route, the one most likely to result in an easy passage. Larocque knew it too, for he'd taken the same route that spring, and for the same reasons – to avoid the Blackfeet. It was only supposed to be Crow in this area, after all, and whites had nothing to fear from them. How was he supposed to know a Cree war party had been in the area?

"Another day and we'll be out of these hills and on the plains between the two mountain ranges," Thin Leg said to the braves, and the men nodded. The Cree were a plains tribe, one used to walking on flat ground. For the past two days they'd been moving through the mountain pass that allowed the Green its swift motion south toward the sea with Mexico, and they didn't much care for it. It often meant rocky mountain trails, the kind that forced the braves to walk single file, sheer drops on either side. Those drops were lessening now that they were coming down the pass's other side, and truth be told it was more hills than anything now. Those heights still rose up from time to time as the landscape rose and dipped, and Larocque knew that if was ever to be a free man again, he'd have to make his move somewhere along their route. For if the Cree got him back to their territory in Canada, the Frenchman knew he was a goner.

Those thoughts were very much on his mind the next afternoon as he and his captors walked along a high ridgeline, one going through the pass between the Absarokas and the Wind River Range. They'd decided to take the high road because Cut Nose had gotten a bad feeling about the trail below, saying something about weird tracks, a Blackfeet band, and the many trails that led through the mountains here. It'd been enough to convince Thin Leg to have them hiking up and up all day, though the Frenchman suspected the Cree chief had since come to regret that decision.

The views were spectacular, that was for sure, with jagged peaks above them and thin canyons below. Pine and spruce rose up all around, each covered in a heavy coating of winter snow. Their route was through such as well, and their footfalls were deep in places. Just in the past hour, however, they'd come to a bit of an overhang produced by the rising mountain walls beside them, and their path was more rocky and bare of snow. It wasn't without threat, however, for the path was narrow and a misstep to either side could have you tumbling down hundreds of feet, likely dying well before you'd hit the bottom far below.

Larocque looked around, for that environment

afforded him many opportunities. Behind him, Thin Leg was bringing up the rear. They were heading up the small ridgeline trail, and ahead of Larocque was Little Pine, his attention set upon the path in front of them, his head down, scanning for rocks or anything else that might trip someone up, send them over the side. He should have been looking behind him.

The Frenchman began moving forward, past Cut Nose and Sand Face. Both looked up at him, and Sand Face spoke up.

"Get back behind us, white dog!"

Larocque ignored him, for he was already a few feet past them by that point, just a few feet from Little Pine.

"Hey!" Thin Leg shouted up at him, but Larocque ignored the brave, even though he expected the man was raising up his bow or tomahawk or something. The Frenchman didn't care, just kept on, now right behind the unsuspecting Cree Indian.

"Little Pine!" he shouted out in the Cree language.

Little Pine spun around at the shout of his name, and Larocque saw the man's eyes go wide in surprise when he spotted him there.

"I told you I'd kill you," the Frenchman said as best he could in Cree, and suspecting that behind him Cut Nose was taking aim with his bow and arrows while Thin Leg took aim with his musket, Larocque grabbed Little Pine by the shoulders. Before the man knew what exactly was going on Larocque spun him around so that he was between himself and the other two braves.

SWISH! SWISH!

"Ugh!"

The Frenchman acted not a moment too soon, for both braves had indeed been aiming, and had indeed been ready to loose. What they hadn't been ready for was their companion being spun around to act as a human shield, and Little Pine's eyes stared back at them in shock and amazement before a thin stream of blood began to run from one corner of his mouth. His body was just beginning to fall forward onto the trail when Larocque grabbed the tomahawk from the brave's limp hand, gripped the haft tightly, and then brought up his arm and let the weapon fly. Head over handle it twirled, its large eagle feathers whipping around in a circle as it sailed out toward the two braves. Both were smart enough to duck down, falling to the ground to avoid the razor sharp weapon. When they looked up, the Frenchman was gone.

25. DROPPING IN

Willow Reed scanned the path before them carefully, for he didn't want to make a bad impression on his first time leading the band. It was a great honor to lead the band in its march for the white, the young brave knew, and he once again thanked his lucky stars that Buffalo Child had chosen him. Well, it'd been Little Mouse that'd picked him over the other two braves that called the Wise One's son their friend. Maybe it was because both Flying Wasp and Small Face had already had that honor, Willow Read thought to himself as he scouted on ahead, but so what? Here he was now, the breeze in his long, black hair and the winter sun shining down. They were walking along the side of the cliffs, heading through the two mountain ranges, westward after the white. So far they'd lost one man, a good one, Buffalo's Child's second in command, and Willow Reed again promised himself that such would not happen during his watch.

The young Indian brave was enjoying that watch when above him, high up on the canyon walls, some pebbles fell. He looked up and saw more pebbles come, then his eyes went wide, for something else was coming down, coming down fast, and right at him.

THUD!

"What was that!" Stone Bear called out from further back on the trail, shouting up at Willow Reed who was in the lead. No answer came, and he looked back toward Buffalo Child and Silver Heart for a moment before breaking into a run. The others were fast on his heels, and then slowing a few moments later. For there the Wise One stood, looking down at the strangest of sights.

"What is it?" Silver Heart called up, but he and the others soon knew as they reached the scene. There before them was Willow Reed, crushed beneath the body of a Cree Indian, blood oozing out from the head of both, though they couldn't see Willow Reed's, for it'd been crushed beneath the Cree. He *was* a Cree, that much was plain from his hair, manner of dress, and bead ornamentation. On top of it he had two snapped off arrows sticking from his chest. Silver Heart turned and looked back at the others.

"What...what..." he managed, at a loss for words. In the back of the group, Small Face could be heard retching. Wolf Calf smirked to that, especially when he looked over at Little Mouse, for the brave was *not* happy at the show of weakness from his companions.

"He fell from above," Buffalo Child said, everyone's eyes going to the group's undeclared leader, "or was pushed." He pointed down at the bodies and then up at the cliffs above. Pebbles still rolled and, as if another Cree might suddenly fall from the heavens upon them, they all silently moved back a few paces.

"What is a Cree band doing this far south, and up on the cliffs above us?" Stone Bear said, but Buffalo Child could only shake his head to that.

"I don't know," he said, looking at them all, "but I intend to find out. Two of those closest to me are now gone, and I mean to find out why."

He pushed past the others, his anger clear, and continued on up the trail, not even looking down at Willow Reed. That bothered his son, Little Mouse, for Willow Reed had been his friend. Wolf Calf saw that clearly, and looked back at his own companions, Quiet Thunder and Running Rabbit. His Skunk Band was now the equal of Little Mouse's Otter Band. *More, for none of my braves are throwing up their breakfast at the first sight of blood.*

He smiled as they started up the trail, Little Mouse and Flying Wasp staying behind to take from Willow Reed's body what they could while waiting for Small Face to regain his composure. The balance of power in the group was changing, Wolf Calf knew, and soon it would be time for him to make his move.

26. ON THE RUN

Larocque ran for all he was worth, used every ounce of strength left in his body, willed himself to press on despite the aches, pains, and sores he was experiencing all over. It was his chest that was giving him the most grief, for he wasn't used to running. Smoking as many peace pipes as he did obviously didn't help matters. He was coughing and wheezing and his lungs were on fire. But onward he ran, up and up the ridgeline and then back down the other side. The Cree Indians were fast on his tail, he knew it, and they wouldn't give up until either he was dead or they'd lost the trail. He knew they wouldn't give up with the latter either, and that he'd likely have to kill them. Still, the rest of their tribe would be out looking for him, and that effectively meant that this area of the country was now closed to the man. *Good,* the Frenchman thought, *it's* well *past time I was in Montreal!*

He was rushing north, up the last dying remnants of the Green River. My the Cree were far outside of their normal area, the Frenchman thought to himself yet again, but there was little time to worry on that. If he was lucky, however, he'd run into some Crow or Shoshone or maybe even the A'anninen. All were tribes at war with the Cree and their Iron Confederacy. The band chasing him was small, only five members, four now that Little Pine was dead, and there was a good chance a few arrows from an opposing tribe would handle this mess for him. Or land him in another, he thought, for there were just as many hostile tribes as there were friendly. He still had to make it up into Canada, and that meant passing by the Blackfeet, Assiniboine, and Chippewa. The last two were part of the Iron Confederacy with the Cree, and if word spread faster than the Frenchman could run, he'd be in big trouble indeed.

Larocque frowned, more because of his predicament than his burning lungs or aching feet this time. He was in trouble, big time, and in an area that didn't look good for him. Being at the northern end of the Wind River Range wasn't exactly the ideal spot. Heading to the west brought him into Blackfeet lands while heading east took him to the Assiniboine lands. Still, west was also the area the Crow called home. And that's the reason the Frenchman turned to his right upon reaching the northernmost point of the Green, where it bent back southward for a time before petering out. He'd go west, toward the Crow, and hope to hell they could save him.

~~~

There! Cut Nose thought to himself as he raced over

the snowy ground. The Frenchman was sneaky, dodging this way and that when he could, jumping over a creek or hopping a bush, all to cover his trail as much as possible. It couldn't really be done in the snow, the Cree tracker knew as he followed the trail, but it could slow a pursuer a few seconds here, a few seconds there, all adding up to enough time for the person to get away. The white wasn't that good, however, and Cut Nose picked up this erratic path easily. It wouldn't matter anyways, not now that the tracker had Thin Leg's musket. He smiled. Any moment now and he'd be upon him, he just knew it.

~~~

Larocque could see the opposing mountain range easily for he was just getting into its foothills. If he could just keep up his pace he'd make it. The problem was how out of shape he was. He hadn't ran or walked much at all during his captivity, and the food he'd been thrown hadn't been much either. All of it was beginning to wear on him, and his energy levels were flagging. He had to keep going though, had to keep...

With a shake of the head he came to, his face in the snow. He'd fallen, he must have fallen, he said to himself as he got up and brushed himself off. He ached all over and his stomach was sending the worst pain up to his head, crying out for food, anything! Larocque ignored it, got up, and kept on.

~~~

"Got you," Cut Nose said quietly to himself when the brave saw the Frenchman stagger up from the snow. He was in bad shape and couldn't keep up the chase much longer. The tracker brought the musket up to his face, took aim, and fired.

BOOM!

~ ~ ~

Larocque's eyes went wide when he heard the shot and wider still a split-second later when the tree beside his head exploded in shards and slivers. He glanced back, saw Cut Nose higher up on a bluff, and took off running, to hell with being tired.

~ ~ ~

Cut Nose swore something fierce as he saw the tree explode beside the Frenchman's head, for the musket ball had missed. He'd never been good with the white man's guns, and he cursed the thing and himself for it. He also cursed himself for leaving his bow and arrows with Thin Leg and Sand Face, and decided right then and there that he'd wait for the two to catch up before chasing the Frenchman further.

27. A COMMOTION

Colter came to a dead stop and behind him Arapoosh did the same. The mountain man put up his hand for silence, and the young brave craned his neck.

"Hear that?" Colter said, not looking back over his shoulder, but keeping his head cocked just so, listening.

Arapoosh listened, but then slowly shook his head. "Hear what?"

"I thought I heard a musket shot," Colter said a moment later, then let out a sigh. "Probably nothing, let's keep moving.

They were moving along the southern reaches of the Absaroka Range, in its foothills, actually. Colter had been adamant that they keep the high ground, something that afforded them a clear view for miles around. So far there were no Blackfeet pursuers, that they could see at least, and that had set Colter's mind at ease. The attack the day before had come as a complete surprise, both to Colter and the Crow. He was still angry at the Indians that'd abandoned him, but he could understand why – this was rough country, the kind that had every man fighting for himself. Every man and boy that was, Colter thought as he glanced back at the young Crow Indian following close behind. He still couldn't believe that he'd run across the young boy, or brave as he insisted on being called, but Colter had a feeling he was lucky for it. The young boy, er...brave, had a way about him, a confidence that Colter rarely saw in men two or three times the lad's age. He'd *have* to be confident, Colter thought to himself, if he heads out and braves these wilds alone. But then he was, for he'd proven that by driving the spear through the Blackfoot pursing Colter.

The mountain man shrugged that thought away and focused on the path ahead of them, snowy and rocky and just waiting for a stray foot to come along so it could have some fun. Colter didn't mean to wind up sliding down one of the hills to the bottom a hundred or more feet below, so he watched his step, and now that he thought he was hearing things, he gripped his rifle a bit more as well.

"Wait!" Arapoosh said, and once again Colter came to a stop on the hilly trail heading through the southern reaches of the Absaroka Range. He was about to turn about and ask what it was, but he didn't have to – there was a commotion coming from the tree line further below, just below the rise of the hills.

Colter looked back at Arapoosh and the two nodded before moving down the hills to check it out.

28. UNBEKNOWNST

"Did you hear that?" Silver Heart said, turning back to the others. Buffalo Child looked skeptical, Wolf Calf saw when he looked up to him, but his father did not and moved forward.

"I heard something, some shouting or something," Stone Bear said. "It sounded like Indians to me, not a white."

"Something's happening around here," Buffalo Child said, "and I think we may have wandered right into it."

"I agree," Silver Heart said. "There's a white out here, but there could be more Crow too. We know there has to be more Cree, and it could be that there are even more whites than we realized. They rarely travel alone, after all."

"One does," Wolf Calf said, speaking up despite

knowing he should not.

Silver Heart looked down at him and frowned. "Then where is he?"

Wolf Calf wouldn't be cowed. "He's ahead of us," the young brave said, "and getting away while we stand here like old women, letting the day slip away as we talk and talk."

That earned a laugh from Buffalo Child, though nothing but a cold look from Stone Bear. He knew his father didn't like his quick temper and tendency to say what he thought, but he couldn't help it. He was about to say just that when Buffalo Child spoke up.

"I like your eagerness, young leader of the Skunk Band," he said, coming up and clapping Wolf Calf on the shoulder, "now show me what that means."

Wolf Calf narrowed his eyes in uncertainly and looked up at the leader of the group.

"I mean, take your braves and go," Buffalo Child said, "go and scout ahead. Track down this white, and if you can kill him. If not call back to us, for we'll be close behind."

Wolf Calf looked from Buffalo Child to his father. The anger was gone from Stone Bear's face, replaced with uncertainty. Wolf Calf knew his father was thinking of an excuse to keep him there, and before he could, the young brave looked to Buffalo Child, nodded, and started off in a run down the trail. A moment later Quiet Thunder and Running Rabbit were doing the same, and suddenly the Blackfeet band was divided in half. Stone Bear looked at Buffalo Child and frowned, but his fellow Wise One only smiled. Buffalo Child knew what he'd done, even if Stone Bear's son had not. Once again, the balance of the group had changed.

29. ALL TOGETHER NOW

Larocque tore through the scrub brush and pushed the tree branches out of his way. He was running and tripping and stumbling at the same time, but he was still ahead of his Cree pursuers, though barely. Any moment now he expected to hear another musket shot, feel the 'whish' of an arrow as it just sailed past, or have his stomach turn over as a tomahawk slammed into a tree just inches from his head. The latter had happened already, a good half an hour before, and the Frenchman had picked up his pace considerably, despite the burning in his chest. Never again would he smoke a peace pipe, he vowed, never again.

Whish...*thunk!*

Larocque's eyes went wide as the arrow embedded itself in the pine tree just inches to his right. He

142

chanced a look back and saw Cut Nose already nocking another arrow to his bow, then Thin Leg rush up beside him and then past, his musket gripped tightly in his hand. The Indians were less than fifty yards behind him now. There would be no recapture this time, the Frenchman knew, for this time the Cree would only settle for his blood, all of it.

Gritting his teeth, Larocque took off running again. He also gripped the half-foot stick in his hand, the one he'd whittled down to a killing point while running, using a sharp rock to do so. As far as weapons went it wasn't much, but it was better than nothing. Larocque just wanted to plunge it into one of his pursuers throats, likely after they'd pumped him full of arrows and were coming in for his scalp. He'd have that satisfaction at least, the knowledge that he took one of the bastards with him.

The Frenchman wasn't ready for that ending just yet, however, and he continued to dash through the trees hoping against hope that the rising elevation of the upcoming hills would slow his pursuers, but somehow not him. He knew it was a wild hope, but that's all he had to cling to. Cling to it he did, and soon he was rushing up the first of the hills that marked the lowest reaches of the Absaroka Range.

~~~

Wolf Calf stumbled and fell down to one knee. Fast behind him came Running Rabbit, and the brave laughed as he moved past. Wolf Calf gritted his teeth and pounded his fist into the snow. He was *not* happy to see his companion move past. That surely meant that he'd bloody his tomahawk first, and Wolf Calf didn't like the thought of that one bit. He was on his feet quickly, and a glance over his shoulder revealed that Quiet Thunder was still a few yards behind. His smile of frustration changed to one of cunning. He could still have the first kill.

~~~

Cut Nose kept his bow tightly at his side, another arrow held ready. He expected to see the Frenchman any moment, for they were off the ridgeline now and in the trees, and this time he wouldn't miss. His view might have been obscured but the ground was flat, and there was nowhere to hide. The man was ahead of them somewhere, he knew it, and pressed onward because of it. Over to his left he heard crashing through the bushes, and the knowledge that his two companions were searching as well only emboldened him to pick up the pace.

~~~

Arapoosh held his spear at the ready, for he'd heard something. Ahead of him, the white did the same, though with his rifle. Something was coming, they both knew it, and they were ready.

Colter had his finger on the trigger of the Northwest Trade gun and he damn-well hoped it didn't misfire this time. He was certain it wouldn't, for he'd cleaned it thoroughly, checked his powder, patches, ramrods...everything. He was ready therefore, and knew it.

Neither the young Crow brave nor the mountain man was prepared for what came tearing through those bushes and trees, however. It was a white man gripping a stick, though with the state of his clothes and emaciated frame, Colter could hardly tell. It was clear right away that the man had been an Indian captive, for Colter had seen a few of them before while growing up in Kentucky as a boy, skeletal and half-crazed figures that'd somehow managed to wander back from the wilderness. This man wasn't that far gone, but he sure looked close.

Larocque had come to a fast halt when he saw the rifle pointed his way, though the sudden rush of relief at seeing a white man holding it was quickly replaced with dread when he saw yet another Indian behind the man, this one obviously having snuck up on him unawares, and now ready to pounce with his spear.

"*Sacrebleu!*" he shouted at Colter, throwing his arm up to point at the young Indian brave, "shoot the bastard!"

Colter lowered his gun a bit from his face. "He's with me," he said to the man, who was clearly French despite his English 'skills,' both from his look and obvious accent.

"*With you?*" Larocque said, his face scrunching up in disbelief. "What do you mean, *with you?* I've got..."

The Frenchman trailed off, and a moment later Colter knew why – there were more crashing noises coming from the trees and bushes from whence he'd come.

~~~

Thin Leg was not happy. First he'd lost a good brave today, for that's what Little Pine had been, a good brave that'd done what he'd been told. He couldn't say the same for Cut Nose, for the tracker had already disappointed him by losing the Frenchman and then in wasting a shot with the musket. He clutched that musket now, for it was loaded and ready to fire once again. *He'd* be the one doing it, too, and raced ahead of the tracker and herbalist, both of whom were a dozen or more yards behind or to his side.

He tore through another set of bushes, expecting another small stretch of ground between the trees before he had to tear through another set still, but instead there was the Frenchman. It wasn't just he, however, but a young Indian boy, as well as another white, one even more haggard and ragged than the first. This one had something that the Frenchman did not, however, and that was death – death in his hands and death in his eyes.

Thin Leg skidded to a stop and brought up his musket. He didn't intend to miss.

~~~

The Indian tore out of the bushes, stopped for a moment, then brought up his musket. Colter saw it all, was expecting it, and had his rifle up and ready. He fired.

BOOM!

~~~

The white man fired first and the shot tore right into Thin Leg's left shoulder, knocking him to the ground, and of course throwing his finger from the trigger. He hit the snow in a daze, not knowing what'd happened.

~~~

"There's more," Arapoosh said as calm as could be, and pointed past the bushes the Indian had just come from. Colter nodded, and didn't let himself worry about the Indian moving around on the ground, moaning and clutching his arm. He got down and started reloading his rifle, then glanced over at the Frenchman. The man was still gripping his stick, his eyes darting every which way.

"Know how to use a pistol?"

The Frenchman nodded and Colter reached into his robes, pulled out Manuel's Harper's Ferry and threw it over.

"Then use it," he said, and nodded toward the bushes. Just then another Indian appeared from them and without hesitation the Frenchman brought the pistol up and fired.

BOOM!

~~~

Wolf Calf came to a stop, looked to his right, and then adjusted his path before running again. Yet another gunshot, this one the second, and just yards away. Then the young Blackfoot brave saw the telltale sign of the weapon's firing, a small cloud of white smoke rising over some scrub bushes and behind some trees. Bringing up his tomahawk, he charged forward, through the bushes, then came to a stop, shocked at what he saw.

He was in a small clearing not more than twenty yards across, and on the other side was Running Rabbit, down on the ground and with blood covering his chest. He was on his back and not moving and Wolf Calf knew he was dead, he just knew it. There was another Indian there, a Cree it looked like, though he was on the ground and grasping his shoulder with a bloody hand. The third Indian was a Crow, even younger than he, and with a spear that he was using to point at Wolf Calf. The young Blackfoot brave had seen that Crow before, and the memory sent chills up his spine.

Wolf Calf's appearance drew the attention of the two white men, one holding a rifle and the other holding a pistol, and both men brought the guns up to point at him. Wolf Calf swallowed the lump in his throat, tightened the grip on his tomahawk, and realized he was going to die. He decided he'd die like a man, and was just about to raise the weapon up and charge forth when a commotion came from yet another side of the clearing, and then another.

~~~

Cut Nose could smell the gun smoke and he slowed as a result. Beside him, Sand Face did not, and the herbalist barreled through the line of bushes, right into what the tracker could only assume was the place where the Frenchman was hiding. With a frown, he started forward too, bringing his bow up for the killing shot he expected to deliver.

~~~

Buffalo Child put his arm up just before the line of tall bushes but it was too late – behind him his son Little Mouse was running too fast, and he and Silver Heart's son Dog Hair tore through the bushes. A moment later Otter Tail and Silver Heart did the same. He frowned. Little Mouse's braves were still rushing up and Wolf Calf and his braves were nowhere to be seen. With a frown, the Blackfeet leader went forth as well.

~~~

Damn! Colter thought when he saw the newest arrival tear through the bushes and into the small clearing. He was little more than a boy, just like the one that the Frenchman had just shot and who now lay dead before them.

Colter's thoughts were taken from that a moment later as another Indian broke through the bushes and came to a stop when he saw them. This one had a bone through his nose and an odd assortment of beads and the mountain man figured he must be a medicine man. A split-second later, from the other side of the clearing, yet another Indian appeared, then another behind him, both boys as far as Colter was concerned. Right behind them, however, came two Indians that were not boys, and then another.

~~~

Little Mouse stopped when he saw the two whites and Crow Indian brave with them, but then his eyes went to Running Rabbit dead on the ground as well as the wounded Cree beside him, *and* the Cree medicine man that'd just jumped through the bushes as well.

"Cree!" he shouted, pointing with his tomahawk toward them. Beside him, Dog Hair brought up his bow.

~~~

Cut Nose heard someone shout "Cree" and his eyes moved from the two whites frantically reloading their guns to the small band of Blackfeet that'd suddenly appeared, one of whom was raising his bow up to fire at Sand Face.

The tracker was still on the other side of the bushes from the clearing, but he had a good view, and a clean shot. Not worrying about the whites, he turned, adjusted his aim, and let loose.

~~~

Dog Hair could feel the arrow's feather fletching on his fingers. He was ready to loose, right at the stunned Cree medicine man.

SWISH!

"Ugh," he managed before looking down to see an arrow sticking from his chest.

He looked back up to see another Cree behind the bushes, one that he somehow hadn't spotted. He began to smile at his stupidity, then started to fall over as life left him.

~~~

"No!" Silver Heart shouted as he tore through the bushes and saw his son take an arrow in the chest. He reached the young brave just as he began to fall to the ground, and caught him just before he hit. He eased him down the rest of the way, staring into his lifeless eyes, the battle around him forgotten.

~~~

"Damn," Colter said as he saw the Indians turn on one another. When the brave with the bow had come out right in front of them, the mountain man had been sure either he or the Frenchman were dead. It was quite the surprise, therefore, when the brave had turned his bow on the Blackfeet that had suddenly appeared.

Colter had no idea what the story was between those two groups of Indians, and he didn't intend to find out. While it'd all been happening the mountain man had not slowed in the loading of his rifle. Flip the cap on the powder horn, pour the powder into the metal charger cup, pour it down the muzzle, reach around for a ball and patch, place the patch down over the top of the muzzle, the ball on top, then the quick starter, a whack of the ball down the barrel, ramrod them down after that, flip the rifle, powder the pan, fire.

BOOM!

~~~

Otter Tail was charging forth with his tomahawk when Colter's rifle ball tore into his chest. The Blackfoot brave was dead before he hit the ground.

~~~

Larocque gave a silent curse at being outraced in his

loading by the mountain man, but that lasted for but a moment before he had his own pan powdered and the 1805 Harper's Ferry pistol ready to go.

~~~

Buffalo Child saw the white load the small gun and bring it up to fire.

"Down!" he shouted at the other two beside him, and then leaped out of the way.

BOOM!

The Frenchman's pistol shot would have hit the Blackfeet leader had he not jumped. Instead the ball shot out at more than a thousand feet per second and took his son Little Mouse in the chest. The young brave went down hard as his father watched in horror.

~~~

Wolf Calf couldn't believe what he was seeing. In the span of just a few seconds, four of his Blackfeet companions were either down or dead, a Cree brave was down with a terrible wound, and the three whites and their Crow friend all still stood in the center of the clearing, unharmed.

A rage boiled up inside the young brave at that, and he gripped his tomahawk and charged forward.

~~~

Cut Nose saw the young Blackfoot that was behind the whites get up and start charging forth. He grabbed another arrow from the quiver on his back and had it nocked. The boy might be a Blackfoot, but he sure wasn't white. Cut Nose knew where his loyalties lay, and it was to his people, not theirs. He took careful aim and promised himself that if he missed it'd only be because he was dead.

~~~

"No!" Stone Bear said as he came to the edge of the bushes and looked at the scene before him. Just then his son Wolf Calf started to rush forward, toward the small group of whites gathered there.

"Cree!" Strong Foot shouted out beside him, and the brave brought up his already-nocked bow and took aim.

~~~

SWISH!

"Ugh!" Cut Nose grunted as something bit him. He still got off his shot.

SWISH!

~~~

Arapoosh watched as the Blackfoot brave charged forth with his tomahawk, an arrow flying just a few inches above the boy's head, but then Arapoosh's attention was jerked to the two Blackfeet that appeared in the bushes behind the boy. One brought his bow and let loose, and Arapoosh turned to watch the arrow sail through the clearing to strike the Cree brave that'd appeared there, the one with the terribly scarred nose. He went down in a heap, though the Cree medicine man beside him was still there, a small knife in his hand.

Arapoosh didn't pay too much attention to that, for he had to jerk back around to avoid the swing of the Blackfoot boy. Arapoosh recognized him, for it was the same boy that he'd seen on the night his brother had disappeared. Whether the brave recognized him or not, Arapoosh had no idea, but he did know one thing – he had to question him about that night, and that meant the boy had to live.

Arapoosh dodged the swing and then the counter-swing that came back. He jumped back yet again as the boy swung, and then one more time. On that last he'd been ready and whipped his spear up and around before slamming its butt into the boy's face.

Blood exploded and Wolf Calf dropped his tomahawk as his hands went reflexively to his face. He stared at Arapoosh through blood soaked hands, his eyes wide with shock.

~~~

Colter saw the blood fly as Arapoosh hit the Blackfoot brave in the face, though he wondered why the young Crow hadn't just killed him. Those thoughts were gone a moment later when Colter saw the remaining Indian in front of them move toward the musket that still lay near the Indian he'd shot in the shoulder.

"There!" he shouted to the Frenchman, pointing at the scene.

"Got it," Larocque said, then brought his arm back and hurled the pistol at the Indian. It hit Sand Face square in the head just as he'd been bending over for the musket, and sent him staggering a few steps.

"What the hell'd you do that for!" Colter shouted.

"What the hell'd you want me to do?" Larocque shouted back. "The gun's empty and I've got no more shots!"

"Then get that musket, damn it!"

"Alright!" Larocque shouted, and lunged forward.

~~~

Further back in the bushes, out of the fight, Flying Wasp and Small Face were watching it all, not believing what they were seeing. They were watching a bit more, too, and that's how they saw the arrow fly from the bushes and strike one of the Crees.

"Crow!" Small Face nearly shouted, and rose up and with his nocked bow, letting loose at the figure he saw there.

"Those aren't Crow, you fool!" Flying Wasp shouted beside him, but it was too late – the arrow was already gone.

~ ~ ~

Stone Bear had a smile on his face, for Strong Foot had just saved his son's life, that was clear. If he'd not fired when he had, the Cree's arrow *wouldn't* have gone inches above Wolf Calf's head, it would have gone inches deep into his chest.

Stone Bear turned to Strong Foot to say just that but stopped cold – his companion was standing there with an arrow through his back, the bloody point sticking out of his chest. Strong Foot looked up from the wound to Stone Bear with a dazed expression, then fell to the ground.

~ ~ ~

Colter knew they had to get out of there, and it was looking like they might have a chance now. That last arrow that'd sailed out had taken the Indian in front of them, and now the Frenchman was going for that musket. To the other side the group of Blackfeet had been reduced in number considerably. Now just two remained, and one seemed to be more interested in one of the dead boys than the fight around them. Behind them the boy that Arapoosh had hit was staggering backward with blood pouring down his face, all while the young Crow brave assaulted him with words in his native tongue too fast for the mountain man to catch, questions it sounded like. That left the spot to his right, the only clear path out of the small clearing. He looked to the Frenchman and shouted.

"Get that gun and let's go!" Then he looked over to Arapoosh. "C'mon!" he shouted, though he doubted the boy heard him at all.

~~~

Got you! Larocque thought to himself as his fingers closed over the musket's barrel and he began to pull it toward him. The wounded Cree Indian laying nearby gave no resistance, so in pain was he from his shoulder wound. The other Cree, however, the medicine man by the look of him, was just starting to recover from the pistol that'd hit him upside the head. Larocque twisted the musket around in his hands and then whistled.

Sand Face turned around to see what the sound was, though his head ached something fierce and he was still seeing stars. His eyes went wide at what he saw next, for there was the Frenchman, and Thin Leg's gun pointed right at him.

"*C'est la vie,*" Larocque said with a smile, *that's life.*
BOOM!

~~~

Arapoosh had turned back at the mountain man's words, and had also looked over at the other white. He'd done so with the latter just in time to see the face of the Cree medicine man blown clean off, though he wished he hadn't – blood and brains flew every which way and splattered the snow-covered trees and bushes on the edge of the clearing. The Crow brave jerked his attention back to the Blackfeet boy that he'd been yelling questions at. His eyes shot to the bushes behind the boy instead, however, for another Blackfoot brave was coming forth, though this one had his eyes on the boy. Somehow Arapoosh knew it was the boy's father, and he also suddenly knew, without a doubt, that it was time to go.

He looked back at the white that'd just fired the musket and saw him getting to his feet, rushing to the mountain man, who was himself running to the edge of the clearing. Across the way, a couple more Blackfeet boys appeared. Arapoosh didn't waste another second and turned about and started rushing toward the whites. He'd have a chance to question the Blackfoot boy later, he'd make sure of that.

PART IV – VENGEANCE

30. TAKING STOCK

Buffalo Child's face was pressed tightly to the shoulder of Little Mouse when he felt a hand on his own shoulder. He didn't know how long he'd been pressed against his son, but he pulled back, eyes closed so as not to look at the boy again, and turned his head before opening them. There behind him was Silver Heart, his own face a mask of sorrow over the son he'd lost as well. Buffalo Child looked past his fellow Wise One and saw the young brave's body there, the arrow still sticking from his chest. He looked back at his own son then, seeing a similar sight, an arrow

protruding from where it should not. Already Little
Mouse's face was losing color.

The Blackfeet leader felt a seething rage rise up in
him at the sight of his son, the sight of Silver Heart
mourning his. He looked around and saw that
Running Rabbit was dead too, as was his own trusted
man, Otter Tail. It'd been a huge loss, this skirmish
with the whites, but some murmuring to his side
reminded Buffalo Child that it hadn't been the whites
alone. He got up, his jaw clenched and his hands
balled into fists, and started toward the source of
those sounds.

On the ground Thin Leg lay still. He'd lost a lot of
blood, he knew, and was feeling weak because of it.
The rifle shot to the shoulder had been a bit closer to
his heart than Colter had realized when he'd fired, and
it'd sapped the Cree leader's strength something fierce.

Buffalo Child knew none of that as he walked up to
the fallen Indian. All he knew was that this band of
Cree was where it shouldn't be, in their territory, or at
least that of the Crow, which was as good as theirs
anyways. Far worse, however, they'd fired on his group
instead of the whites. It didn't matter to Buffalo Child
that his Blackfeet had shouted out to fire on the Cree
first, for all he knew was that his son was dead, and
someone had to pay.

He reached Thin Leg and bent down, putting his
face close to the wounded brave's. "What are you doing
here?" he asked in their shared Algonquin dialect.
Thin Leg only moaned in response, a pitiful sound that
an old woman would utter while making water. Buffalo
Child smacked him across the face a few times. "Who
are the whites?" he asked next.

"French..." Thin Leg managed, his eyes beginning to
cloud over, "Frenchman."

Buffalo Child nodded and looked back at the others,
all of them gathered around now. There were just
seven of them now, including himself, where before

there'd been twelve. "French trappers that have come too far south," he said to them, "and ones we'll teach a lesson to."

With that he turned back to the wounded Cree, glanced around at the trampled-down snow around them, and reached for a sizeable rock.

"Tell your ancestors what a Blackfoot's anger tastes like," he bent down and whispered into Thin Leg's ear, then brought the stone up and smashed it down on the Cree's face, again, and again, and again...

He only stopped when he felt another hand on his shoulder. Turning around he saw Stone Bear and the others looking at him strangely.

"Time to go home," the Wise One said.

Buffalo Child looked at the others, his eyes narrowing, his face covered in the Cree's blood. *"Go home!* Why, we've got two whites and a River Crow to kill!"

"No!" Stone Bear said with a calm voice despite the power he'd put behind it. "We're not going to lose anymore young braves or strong warriors because of your hate."

"I agree," Silver Heart said.

"I can't believe I'm hearing this!" Buffalo Child shouted as he started to get up. He reached down and grabbed a stray tomahawk that was lying there. "Silver Heart, you just lost your son, the second that you've lost to these whites in little more than a year. You want to go back and just let them get away with that!"

"I've lost Otter Tail too," Silver Heart said, motioning toward the dead brave's body, "just as you lost Slow Breeze in the canyons. We've both lost a son, and that's enough."

"Enough? Enough you say?" Buffalo Child said with a laugh. "Fine, then you cowards head home, back to the village to wait the winter out with the old men and the hags. Go!" He looked at the others for a few moments, and noticed the young braves shifting

nervously behind the two Wise Ones. "Flying Wasp...Small Face," he said, and the two braves looked up, "what say you to this idea of going home?"

"Uh..." Small Face said, for he was still expecting to be punished at any moment for killing Strong Foot with his misplaced arrow. So far that hadn't been found out, however, and he meant to keep it that way.

"I don't want to go home," Flying Wasp said, cutting in when it was clear his companion was at a loss for words.

"Good, then you can come with me," Buffalo Child said, waving the boys over. Both started to come.

"No," Silver Heart said, stepping forward, "I won't let these young braves get caught up in your suicidal vengeance quest!"

"And how are you going to stop me?" Buffalo Child said, a twisted smile coming to his face.

Silver Heart took in a deep breath, surprised at what he was hearing. It was clear that Chief He Who Shouts had been right not to name Buffalo Child as his successor. He took a step forward, meaning to grab the two braves by the wrists and drag them from the clearing, all the way to the Blackfeet village if necessary, but he never got that far. Buffalo Child drew back his arm and then hurled it forward, letting the tomahawk fly. It struck Silver Heart in the chest and embedded itself deeply. The force of the blow knocked the Wise One from his feet and he fell on his back hard, something that knocked the wind out of him.

"What are you doing!" Stone Bear shouted as he rushed toward the Wise One, who was still sucking for breath despite the terrible wound he'd suffered.

"Taking charge of this band," Buffalo Child said as Stone Bear reached Silver Heart.

Stone Bear didn't know what to do, for Silver Heart's wound was too deep, and the man seemed to know that, for he stopped trying for breath and allowed himself to slip away. Stone Bear moved his hand up and closed the man's eyes, then turned an angry face to Buffalo Child.

"He Who Shouts will hear of this!" he said, standing up and facing his fellow Wise One.

"How are you going to reach him?" Buffalo Child asked with a grin. "With your son and his brave?"

Stone Bear glanced back at Wolf Calf and Quiet Thunder. He didn't want to put them in harm's way, and anything having to do with Buffalo Child would be in harm's way. He turned back to the Wise One, who was clearly becoming anything but. "Let us go."

"When the whites are dead," Buffalo Child replied.

A tense silence followed as the two Wise One's stared at one another, neither wanting to break their gaze first. Finally Stone Bear let out a sigh, looked down, and nodded.

"Fine," he said, "but know that when the whites are dead, we go our separate ways."

"As you wish," Buffalo Child said, and began to walk away. Flying Wasp and Small Face gave their peers confused looks before hustling after him.

Stone Bear turned back to his son and Quiet Thunder. "We'll get through this," he said, "I don't know how, but we'll get through this."

He rose and began to follow the others, but behind him Wolf Calf hesitated for a moment before following. He wasn't so sure his father was right.

31. HIGH-TAILING IT

Colter rushed through bushes, around the trees, over the gullies, and through the creeks. He dodged low-hanging branches and jumped over larger rocks. Dips in the ground were leapt over and rises climbed quickly, all of it, of course, in the snow. He was running, and behind him he could hear the Frenchman doing the same. Whether the young River Crow Indian was still with them he wasn't sure, but when he'd glanced back ten minutes or so earlier, he'd caught a glimpse of him way back in the trees.

The mountain man ran and ran and would have kept on running all day had not the Frenchman started coughing and wheezing and carrying on something fierce. Finally the man shouted "enough!" and Colter was forced to stop when he heard the sounds behind him lessen. He turned back to see the Frenchman standing there, bent over with hands on knees, coughing his lungs out or near enough. The mountain man scoffed and started back, just as Arapoosh came crashing in behind them.

"C'mon," Colter said, "they could be right behind us, and likely will be even if they're taking their time – our trail is obvious!" They were in thick trees, with little more than five feet or so between them, bushes and rocks scattered all over and covered with snow, the better to trip them up.

"I can't...go...no further," Larocque managed, coughing up another gob of phlegm for his efforts.

"I don't think they're following close behind," Arapoosh said. His own breathing was labored, but he wasn't a smoker like the Frenchman. "I stopped a few times to see, but–"

"Stopped!" Colter cried out. "What did you do that for? Are you *trying* to get killed!"

"No, I'm trying to figure out what happened to my brother!" Arapoosh shouted back, close to tears. He was exhausted, sleep-deprived and hungry on top of it. The stress of the fight and now being yelled at weren't helping things. Colter seemed to sense this, for he held back.

"Just give me a minute," Larocque said. "I can...I can...I..."

And with that the Frenchman fell over and landed in the snow. He wasn't hurt, just exhausted, and a look of relief spread across his face as he lay there.

Colter shook his head but didn't complain too much – the stop gave him a chance to reload his rifle. That took twenty seconds and seeing that the Frenchman hadn't recovered in that time, he gestured for the man to throw him the pistol, which he did. Colter had that loaded just as quick and was standing again.

"C'mon!" he said. "Those Blackfeet aren't going to let us get away so easily – let's get out of here."

"Alright, alright...just give me a minute," Larocque began, but Colter gave him a few seconds, the amount of time it took him to walk over and heft the Frenchman to his feet. The look of surprise on Larocque's face was quickly replaced by one of dislike, but he swallowed his pride and started after the man. Arapoosh just shook his head to it all and took up the rear, glancing over his shoulder occasionally for the Blackfeet that he hoped were coming.

32. A NEW COMPANION

No Blackfeet came, that day or into the next. The three companions started up the valley on the western face of the Absarokas. It was lush country in summer but snow covered it all now. Buffalo and elk wandered by, as did the occasional wolf. The three travelers eyed the latter but dared not hunt the former – any sign of their passing was the last thing they wanted. All they could hope was that snow would come each night, wiping out that day's tracks.

Most often it didn't however, and the men trudged on, out into the wide valley and toward the other distant mountain range, the one that had the Snake River flowing by. That'd lead them back to the Yellowstone, Larocque had said, and that was just fine by Colter, as he'd have an easy go of it back to the fort once he reached the river.

Francois Antoine Larocque was the Frenchman's full name, Colter had learned over their time together, for there wasn't much to do while walking save look and talk, and Larocque was quite good at talking. That's how he'd learned that they'd met once before. The mountain man had *thought* he looked familiar.

It'd all started when Colter asked him how he'd come to be out in the middle of nowhere, though he'd quickly regretted asking the question – the man would *not* shut up!

"Got my start because of my uncle, Laurent Leroux, who was one of the earliest trappers with Gregory, MacLeod and Company," the Frenchman told him.

Colter had nodded, for he'd heard of the British fur trapping company, one that sent men out quite far, and for quite some time. They operated all over Canada and quite a bit in the Pacific Northwest, the mountain man knew, and were quite the thorn in the North West Company's side.

"How'd they do against the Hudson's Bay Company?" Colter asked.

"Not too good," Laroque said, "but then no one can do too well against them, what with how much of western Canada they control. That's why we have to move ever further toward the Pacific, further into America. That's what my uncle did, and he mainly focused on the far reaches of the Northwest Territory, right up to the Arctic Ocean. In fact, it was he that started the first trading post way up north on Great Slave Lake."

"Thought that was Alexander Mackenzie?"

Laroque nodded. "Oh, it was, it was...he and my uncle were travelling together."

Colter nodded. He'd never heard of the lake, but Laroque had that self-assured smile on his face, the one Colter was getting quite used to. When the man had that look, the mountain man knew it was best just to humor him and nod along with whatever was being said.

"Unfortunately," the Frenchman continued with a sigh, "the boss of Gregory, Macleod and Company was murdered and the company combined with the North West Company. My uncle would hang on for a few more years before getting into banking in Montreal. After that, his trapping days were done."

"When was that?"

"Around 1792, well before my time," Laroque said. "Didn't get my start until then, for that's when I left my native Quebec and headed to America. Didn't know a smidgen of English when I got here, though I can thankfully say that's changed."

Colter looked up at the smiling Frenchman, and wasn't so sure – with an accent as thick as that Colter often thought he should carry a knife around just to cut the air.

"Wasn't until 1804 that I joined up with the XY Company on the Assiniboine River," Laroque continued. "A short time after that the North West Company took the small company over and I soon was working for the competition it seemed." He sighed. "Didn't much matter to me – I just wanted to get out to trade and trap."

"And that's how you ran into the Captains," Colter said.

"That's how I ran into the Captains," Laroque repeated with a nod. "It was the end of November 1804 and you were all wintering with the Mandans for the first time."

"Aye," Colter said, "I remember it well now. You wanted to go with us west, but the Captains wouldn't allow it."

"Don't blame 'em too much – would you want a French trapper that was working for the British to find out all your trade routes?"

Colter smiled. "Not like you could have found 'em

anyways – Captain Lewis had to repair your compass!"

"*Oui, oui,*" Laroque said with a frown that quickly turned into a smile, he had a tendency to speak in his native tongue when he was flustered or angry or outdone, "well, you know how it is."

"I think what it really was were your journals," Colter said.

"Oh?"

The mountain man nodded. "I have it on good authority that both Captains Clark *and* Lewis were disappointed after having read the journals; it made the two realize how drab their own writing was by comparison."

"I'd imagine – I bed down and live with the tribes I visit, especially the Hidatsa and Mandan, while you Americans hold yourselves so aloof."

Colter had nothing to say to that one, for the Frenchman was right and he knew it.

After that their talk had turned to the predicament at hand. They had the conversation that day over a lunch of pemmican and dried berries, the Snake River not too far off in the distance.

"So what do you think we should do?" Larocque said, looking at the mountain man. Colter let out a sigh, walked a few feet away, and rubbed at his beard. After a minute of thought he turned back.

"What do you think?" he asked the Frenchman, though he also darted his eyes over to Arapoosh. "You've been around this area – what's the best way for us to get away."

The Frenchman shook his head while brushing some snow off a large rock. "I'm not sure we can get away," he said as he sat down. "We killed a lot of Blackfeet back there, and they're likely not happy about that. And I don't know about you, but quite a few of them looked awfully young to me. If one was a son, we'll never get away."

"So we fight," Arapoosh said, banging his spear

against his small shield. The two men looked over at the boy, then each other.

Colter shrugged. "What else are we to do then?"

"Nothing," Larocque said, "we're not going to get away from them, all we can do is find the most favorable area to make a stand."

"So where's that?"

Larocque nodded his head toward the river. "Further north, where the Snake drains into the wastelands of the Yellowstone."

"*Yellowstone?*" Colter said. "Does it start this far south?"

"That it does," Larocque said, now motioning at the western mountains to their right. "She starts in the Absarokas here before passing through the Snowy Mountains and another range to the west of them, then circles back up onto the course you were likely on last winter. Your fort shouldn't be more than 150 miles downriver at that point."

"An easy jaunt in a dugout," Colter said, and Larocque nodded.

"You could be back by the first buds of spring, probably sooner."

Colter took in a deep breath and turned back to look at the Snake. The river was twisting its way northward just as its name implied. Already they'd passed one large lake at the foot of the jagged peaks that bordered the region, and now the spruce and fir and juniper were appearing more frequently, stark shades of green against the vast winter wonderland of white that assaulted them from every direction. Only the big sky above offered another respite, it's blueness as infinite and unknown as ever.

"Let's do it then," Colter said, turning back around to look at Larocque and Arapoosh. The young River Crow brave nodded at his words, while the Frenchman clapped his hands down on his knees and stood up from his rock.

"Alright," he said, beginning to rub his hands together. He then bent down and drew a few lines in the snow, grabbed a few stray rocks, and started to draw a rudimentary map.

"Up ahead we'll run into a large lake, what the Crow call Yellowstone Lake. After that there are bubbling pools, cauldrons of steaming mud, and a great waterfall once the river picks up again." He looked up at them. "It's at the waterfall that we'll make our stand."

33. FOLLOWING THE SNAKE

Wolf Calf was looking up at the jagged peaks of the Teton Mountains, or at least what was left of them. They'd passed the large lake at their base more than a day ago and were nearing Yellowstone Lake and the strange lands that surrounded it. Beside the young Blackfoot brave was Quiet Thunder, and once again Wolf Calf looked over and clapped him on the shoulder.

"It'll be alright," he said quietly, leaning in close. Buffalo Child was only a dozen or so yards ahead of them on the trail, and the young leader of the Skunk Band didn't want the Wise One, or the remaining two members of the Otter Band, to hear him.

Quiet Thunder nodded. "I'm scared, Wolf Calf..." he trailed off and shook his head. "Running Rabbit...Little

Mouse...Dog Hair...they weren't supposed to die."

"I know," Wolf Calf said, and he looked up at his father. As if reading his mind, Stone Bear turned and looked over his shoulder at them. Something in their faces must have convinced the man to try again, for he frowned and moved up the trail further, getting closer to the group's leader.

"Buffalo Child," he called out, "stop!" Ahead, the Wise One kept up his steady pace as if he'd not heard. Stone Bear firmed up his face and shouted out again. "Stop and–"

"And what?" Buffalo Child shouted out at Stone Bear as he wheeled about, slapping his new musket down in his hands. Most of the powder the Cree had had on him had been wet, but some had not, and the Wise One knew he could count on the gun for a few shots, at least. "Do you intend for me to run back to the tribe, run back like some cur with its tail between its legs?" he laughed. "That's you, Stone Bear, not I."

Wolf Calf looked up at his father, saw the anger in his face, an anger held in check...for now. And how could it not be? Buffalo Child was on a death mission, one that'd likely result in his death and any that were around him. Whether that death would result in the death of his intended prey, the two whites and their strange Indian ally, Wolf Calf had no idea, nor did he intend to find out. Like his father, he knew they had to get away. Looking over at the remaining two braves of the Otter Band, boys really, he now thought for the first time, for that's all they were really, boys far from home and scared because of it. He could see that fear in Small Face's eyes especially, though Flying Wasp still stood with his chest puffed out, his pride evident. He fully expected an easy victory over the whites, as did Buffalo Child, and Wolf Calf knew this would cost them dearly, cost them all.

"We will continue to follow you, Buffalo Child," Stone Bear said with a sigh, then shaking his head, "though I know folly lies down that path."

"But follow me you will, my fellow Wise One, for you know it'll be a greater folly should you return back to the village and the dying man we still for some reason call 'chief.' If that should happen, your folly will mean your death."

The two men stared daggers at one another for a few more moments before Buffalo Child scoffed, wheeled about, and continued up the trail, following the Snake River as it twisted and turned ever northward to the strange lands there.

"Come Flying Wasp and Small Face," he called out with a smile, waving them on with the musket, "we've two whites to kill and a River Crow dog!"

The two braves looked from Buffalo Child back to Stone Bear, Wolf Calf, and Quiet Thunder, and then headed up the trail as well.

"Father–"

"Walk," Stone Bear said, cutting off his son.

The young brave frowned, but did as he was told.

34. THE SKY PEOPLE

The wind howled and snow swirled, and the world around them was dark. It was about as cold as could be, Colter figured, and the three huddled together under a small defile of rock shivering against the wind. No fire had been set, for something like that would immediately tip off the Blackfeet following them. They'd reached Yellowstone Falls just as dusk was coming in, and night quickly followed. Both Arapoosh and Larocque had ensured the mountain man that the falls were there, even though he couldn't hear them.

"Frozen," Larocque had told him, "though if you listen carefully, you might be able to pick up a bit of water that's not, for there's always something running under the surface."

Colter had listened, for quite some time, but all he'd

picked up was a faint droning sound, like a bee that'd been caught in some back room. He'd have to wait until morning to see, and that couldn't come soon enough, he thought, as he sat and huddled with the others.

The night passed slowly, with the men huddled together. For Arapoosh, however, this was nearly unbearable. The Blackfeet were out there, and one in particular had the answers he sought. He'd spoken of the Sky People and Above World before with the two men, Colter in particular. The mountain man had scoffed at him, but what Arapoosh hadn't know was that Colter had a sneaking suspicion he *already* knew about these Sky People, and had since that night he and Forest had been out, rushing back to the cave from the A'anninen village. He'd asked Arapoosh about that night, and about that village, but the young brave had only shaken his head, saying it was likely Colter had stayed at one of the many A'anninen villages that dotted the area around the Yellowstone River, and that it was just as likely gone by now, for that was the way of the Indians. He hadn't shaken his head about the strange light that Colter had seen in the sky, however, indeed, that's when he'd become much more interested in the mountain man.

"What did it look like...where was it going...did it tell you anything?"

Those were all questions the young brave had shot Colter's way on their journey so far, but the mountain man had only shaken his head and said he hadn't a clue. That perturbed Arapoosh, but only for a few moments. After that he nodded and launched into a lengthy explanation of the Sky People and Above World, as he called them. He did so again that night while the three huddled amidst the rocks.

"They come in giant canoes of the sky," Arapoosh said, his teeth chattering against the wind as the mountain man pressed closer to him, the better to share their warmth, "and sometimes they land." He shook his head. "I haven't seen them myself, a landing I mean, but I've heard stories. The ships are large, circular, and have openings you can't see. The Sky People, when they do come out, are tall and white...whiter than you!" He said that last with a smile. "No hair, however, "Arapoosh was firm to note, "not a hair on their bodies."

"What do they want?" Colter asked, going along with the tail. He could understand shooting stars looking like canoes in the sky, but to actually see one land and people get out? That was a bit much.

"We're their children," Arapoosh said matter-of-factly, "and they watch over us, and the animals as well. Many times members of my tribe and others have found buffalo that have been cut up, pieces taken out." He frowned. "Always cut and taken out in a way that no knife ever could."

"Don't sound like 'watching over' to me," the Frenchman scoffed, his teeth beginning to chatter as well. Outside their small overhang of rock the snow was swirling in the frigid wind.

"Oh, they are," the brave said, "they are. They look to the animals and what they eat, studying them to make sure that what *we* eat is safe as well. Like I said, we're their children and they watch over us, always have and always will."

A few moments of silence fell after that, for Arapoosh had winced slightly and Colter had noticed. He knew why, too – the brave was questioning his own words. After all, Colter had already learned that the reason the boy was out in the wilderness on his own was because he was looking for his brother, doing so under the guise of a vision quest. The Sky People had taken his brother, he claimed, and he meant to get him back or find out why. *Or die trying*, Colter thought.

Once again the mountain man wondered just how

much these Sky People really *were* watching over, and how much they were using the tribes like prey. That's when he made himself believe the tales at all, which wasn't often, and then usually before he shook his head and muttered something like, "get your head together, John."

Both he and Laroque muttered something to that effect now, and the three settled back into silence. The wind howled and swirled around them, and they huddled down, bracing themselves against the cold.

~~~

A shooting star streaked across the clear sky, *or was it a star?* That's what Arapoosh thought as he watched it quickly appear and then disappear, a sight he'd seen many times. He took it as the signal he'd been waiting for and slowly began to get up. Beside him the Frenchman and the mountain man slept, both snuggled tightly into the furs of the other. Larocque didn't have a coat, but Colter had quite a few furs he'd picked up on his trek, and the Frenchman had been thankful for them. "And you'll be paying for 'em if they come back to me smelling like that Paris foo-foo water!"

"It's called *cologne*," Laroque had said, "and would probably increase their value, at least with the fine Parisian women, though I'd expect you wouldn't know anything about that, eh?"

Arapoosh smiled at the memory of the men talking, and was once again thankful that he'd spent so much time huddled outside the medicine man's tent back in the village when the other trappers had come through over the years. He'd picked up a lot of the white man's talk, and knew he probably wouldn't be alive right now had he not.

Now standing, Arapoosh took another look at the men. They hadn't been disturbed by his motions and he moved away, out into the night, southward toward the band of Blackfeet he knew to be close.

35. A VISIT

Wolf Calf awoke and saw that the snow was still swirling outside the small cave they'd found. It wasn't so much a cave as a small cleft in the mountain, but it'd kept a bit of the wind's bite off. Off of Buffalo Child and the two braves that followed him at least, for that's about all the room it had. Wolf Calf looked up at the three now, sleeping inside, while just outside were his father and Quiet Thunder. The young Blackfoot brave frowned at the situation but didn't dwell on it – he had to make water and the sooner he did that the sooner he could be laying down again, hopefully to fall asleep and awake when the sun was shining.

Wolf Calf moved out past the first few trees and then

came to a stop, started to relieve himself. He was doing that still when a hard object was suddenly beneath his chin, pushing it up.

"The slightest of moves and that throat is cut," Arapoosh said from the darkness behind the Blackfoot.

Wolf Calf gulped but that was it. A moment later he saw the River Crow boy appear before him, though the spear was still held beneath to his throat.

"You never answered my questions," Arapoosh said, referring to the day they'd met in the clearing where the skirmish had taken place.

Wolf Calf said nothing and a moment later Arapoosh lowered the spear, though only slightly.

"I don't know what you're talking about, I–"

The spear was back up under his chin and the brave stopped talking.

"You were out there that night, out amidst the blackness, I saw you. There were eight of you, all on horseback, painted ponies with handprints and streaks, yellow, red and white. The braves were nestled in buffalo furs, and seemed to be making a slow pace, not rushing at all. That's when the light appeared in the sky."

Wolf Calf said nothing, just stared at the young boy. He was speaking the truth, for he *had* been out that night with Silver Heart and some of the Otter Band. Calf Looking had invited him and both of their fathers had said it'd be alright. That was when he and Sidehill Calf were still alive, something that seemed so long ago now.

"Ah-ha," Arapoosh said, smiling, for he could see the recognition in the young brave's eyes, could see that his words were registering as truth.

"What of it?" Wolf Calf said, spat was more like it, and the spear point dug up a bit into his chin for his efforts.

"I lost my brother that night, Thrown into the

Spring, taken right from beside me. The Sky People took him," he said, looking up for a moment. Wolf Calf caught that look and narrowed his eyes. "They came right down from Above World in their canoes of the sky, came right down and took him." He glanced up again. "I mean to find out what happened, and I mean to find out what you–"

Arapoosh had just started to glance back at Wolf Calf when the young Blackfoot made his move. His hand shot up and latched onto the spear just below the point, pushing it away from him. Arapoosh was caught off guard by the move and by the time he could thrust upward, Wolf Calf's chin was long gone.

"Father! Father!" the young Blackfoot brave shouted as he ran back toward the rocky cleft they'd been sleeping under.

Arapoosh saw him go and raised his spear up for a killing throw. He held the weapon, but didn't release. The Blackfoot *had* been there that night, and likely *had* seen what had happened. Killing him wouldn't bring back Thrown into the Spring, and neither would his own death. On the third shout of "father" the young Crow brave turned and ran, hoping he could get back to the whites before the six Blackfeet could catch him.

36. RUDE AWAKENING

Colter awoke with a start, though if you'd asked him why he couldn't have said. The sky was still dark though lightening quickly. Dawn wasn't far off, though the air still held a chill bite and a light snow had begun. The wind, thankfully, had died off. That wasn't what had awoken him, however, and looking over to his right he quickly found a reason not to care what the reason had been – Arapoosh was gone.

"Larocque," he said, shaking at the Frenchman who was still asleep to his left, "wake up!"

"Hm...wh...what?" Larocque said as he started to come to. He looked over and saw that the young Indian boy was gone then saw Colter's wide eyes. He knew immediately that something was wrong.

"He's gone," Colter said, standing up now.

"Maybe he's just in the trees taking care of business," Larocque said as he pulled the myriad small furs closer to him.

"I don't think so," Colter said, "for his things are gone. Besides, he..."

The mountain man trailed off and Larocque narrowed his eyes, looked back up at him. "What is it?" he said, but Colter's hand shot up and silenced him.

"Hear that?" he said a moment later.

The Frenchman leaned forward a bit. That's when he heard the whoops and hollers coming from the south.

~~~

"Whoop! Yip! Whoo!"

The shouts came to Arapoosh, for he was only a few dozen yards ahead of them. They were Blackfeet shouts, those given by young braves on the warpath. It was early but on the warpath they were, for a young River Crow had come into their camp and they weren't going to let him get away with it.

Arapoosh dashed this way and that, hoping he could keep up the pace and reach the two whites before his pursuers caught up. Already they'd gained considerable ground on him since the young brave had slipped past his spear. On the trek out he'd been worried the Blackfeet had been too close, but now he was wishing they'd been closer.

Onward he ran, and just as an arrow sailed past him, several feet to his left. It was the first he'd seen, however, and that meant there'd be others. The Blackfeet were gaining on him, and he still had quite a ways to go.

~~~

Buffalo Child saw Small Face's arrow go wide and he cursed silently to himself. Slow Breeze never would have missed that shot, but the Wise One's companion was dead now, as were most of them, his son too. The thought of Little Mouse fueled the anger inside of Buffalo Child and he plowed on through the snow and over the rocks, following the River Crow's footprints.

~~~

"Something's tearing through those trees," Larocque said as he hurried up, the furs forgotten at his feet. He clutched the pistol Colter had given him, looking down every few seconds to make sure it was still ready to fire.

"Yep," Colter said. He had his Northwest Trade gun up at his face, pointed, and ready to fire at whatever might come up the small rise between the trees that led to their position.

"Blackfeet, it's got to be the Blackfeet," Larocque said.

"Yep," Colter said.

"Damn it, man!" Larocque said, looking to the mountain man now and not out into the trees. "Aren't you worried about–"

"Colter, Colter, Colter!" came a cry from below them, through those trees that Colter had his gun trained on. It was Arapoosh's voice, they both recognized it, and the mountain man lowered his rifle just as the boy appeared.

"Where have you–" Larocque began to say, but Arapoosh paid him no mind and began talking to Colter.

"Six," he said between panting breaths, "six Blackfeet. Coming this way. One with a musket."

Colter nodded, clapped the boy on the shoulder, and ferried him up toward the Frenchman. "Go," he said, "go and wait for me at the falls."

"What are you going to do?" Larocque said as the young boy began to drag him away.

"You'll hear soon enough," the mountain man said, and then they were gone, up the mountain and to the falls.

37. ON THE PATH

Flying Wasp did as his name implied – he flew up the mountain rise, through the trees, and over the rocky ground. He wasn't flying, Buffalo Child saw as the young brave went past, but he was running fast. The Wise One smiled. Here was a young Blackfoot that knew how to prove himself!

Flying Wasp was trying to do just that – prove himself. He knew that Buffalo Child was right to seek the killers of his son, and that Stone Bear was wrong for opposing him. He just hoped he had a chance to prove himself in battle, had a chance to show that when Buffalo Child took over for Chief He Who Shouts, Flying Wasp was one he'd want by his side. Perhaps he could even become like a son to the Wise One, something that would be easy since his own father had been killed in a skirmish with the Crow years ago.

Those thoughts were on the Blackfoot brave's mind when he went up the rocky rise that the River Crow's footsteps showed him, and that's when he ran into quite the shock.

~~~

Colter was waiting for a brave to fly up the small incline at him, but not a boy. Nonetheless, he fired upon the first sight of movement and the rifle kicked to life.

BOOM!

The ball tore forth at more than a thousand feet per second and ripped into Flying Wasp's chest, shattering his sternum and sending a bone shard into his heart. The young brave was dead before his head hit the ground.

~~~

Buffalo Child frowned, for he knew what'd just happened and didn't need to see – the white was up ahead, had seen Flying Wasp come at him, and hadn't hesitated. The Wise One brought up his musket and barreled ahead, knowing the man would be desperately reloading or already running away. Either way, Buffalo Child would kill him.

~~~

Colter was rushing up the incline, following the foot tracks of Larocque and Arapoosh, when he heard movement behind him. He immediately dropped down to the ground and was lucky for it.

BOOM!

The musket shot tore into the tree just a few feet ahead of him, and would have torn into his back had he not fallen when he had. He rolled over on his stomach, saw the Blackfoot that'd fired the musket, and started to get up. The Indian was staring death at him, but he was also stopping to reload the gun, something he wasn't that good at, the mountain man saw. At that rate he'd get another shot off in forty seconds, not the usual twenty. Colter got up and started running.

~~~

Buffalo Child swore under his breath, but kept up his reloading. A few moments later Small Face came up behind him, and the brave stopped when he saw his dead friend lying there.

"He killed Flying Wasp," Buffalo Child said, not taking his eyes from the musket, but flicking his chin up the path, "go."

Small Face had his doubts, but he also had an anger rushing into him, one brought on by the sight Flying Wasp lying there dead. He gritted his teeth and gripped his tomahawk and took off up the hill. He'd almost disappeared through the trees when Stone Bear and Wolf Calf arrived on the scene.

"Enough," Stone Bear said angrily when he saw the dead brave lying there, "enough. How many more have to die, Buffalo Child, for you to be happy? *All of us?*"

"No," Buffalo Child said as he finished loading the musket and twirled it up as he too rose, "just the whites."

With that he was rushing up the path after Small Face.

38. THE FALLS

Colter tore up the path and came to the rise, there below him twenty feet was the Yellowstone River, frozen over and covered with white snow. His eyes went down to the ground at his feet and the footprints there, Larocque's and Arapoosh's, leading down to the river and then off to the left. Colter started down the hill and was soon skidding. He didn't mind – the sound of someone rushing behind him was quite clear now, and he fully expected the Blackfoot brave's musket was now loaded. He reached the riverbank and ran.

~~~

"There he is," Larocque said, his left hand going up

to point, "there's Colter."

Arapoosh turned back from the top of the falls and saw that it was true – the mountain man was rushing down the riverbank and then out onto the frozen ice. You had to in order to make it past the rock overhangs that jutted out before the falls began.

Colter jumped around those rocks and then came to a stop. He could hear the sound of water running, but it certainly wasn't rushing like a waterfall should sound like. Then he saw it, the falls, frozen over completely, not even a thin trickle going down. He was still moving quickly and nodded at Larocque and tousled Arapoosh's hair as he passed by them, for he had to get as close to the edge as he could, had to see what more than a hundred feet of falling water looked like when it was frozen. Leaning out over as far as he dared, the mountain man was struck by the hundred-foot column of ice that went from the canyon floor to his position high above. It wasn't really a hundred feet, though, he saw, for the water had frozen upward into drifts several dozen feet from where it struck, creating a patchwork of jagged hills and troughs of ice fifty yards down the lower portion of the river.

Colter took it all in for but a moment before turning his attention back behind him. "Five," he said, looking to Larocque especially, for he had a pistol, "five are left."

"You got one, eh?" the Frenchman nodded, looking back. "Good, that'll–"

His words were cutoff as an arrow sailed out and skipped off the rock wall jutting out near his head. If he'd been leaning a few inches further out, he'd have been dead. The shock and surprise of the arrow threw the Frenchman back and he stumbled, started to fall, and would have had he not released his grip on the pistol to save himself. The gun flew backward, hit the ice of the river, and skidded towards the edge.

Larocque looked from the gun to Colter, his eyes

wide. The mountain man narrowed his eyes and cocked his head at the man. With a deep breath, Larocque started for the gun.

~~~

Stone Bear's arrow had missed, but then he hadn't really put much heart into the shot. His heart wasn't in this fight, not like Buffalo Child's was, and the Wise One held back as the blood-crazed leader of the Otter Band rushed forth, Small Face close on his heels. Beside him, Wolf Calf looked on, not sure what he should do, not sure if his father would let him break loose and join in the fight. He wanted to, he wanted to badly.

~~~

Arapoosh watched as Larocque dove for the gun and then turned his attention back to Colter. The mountain man was aiming his rifle right at the Blackfoot brave that was rushing forth. He was holding a musket, but for some reason, wasn't using it. Then Arapoosh knew why.

~~~

Colter didn't wait another second, for the Blackfoot warrior was too close – he aimed and fired.
BOOM!

~~~

Buffalo Child had been expecting the shot, had known it was coming. That's how he was able to go into a slide at just the right moment. The rifle fired and the ball went over his head, by a few hairs it felt like. He put his foot into the ground hard and came up, his own gun ready to fire. He got on one knee and took aim and pulled the trigger.

BOOM!

~~~

Colter saw right after his shot that the Indian had been expecting him to fire, and was ready. That's why he started to pull away right after firing, hoping it'd be enough.

The Indian's musket fired and the ball flew a hair from his chest, or so it felt. His back slammed into the rock wall of the upper canyon and he was just about to push himself off of it when he looked up and saw the Blackfoot rushing at him.

Buffalo Child slammed into Colter, for he'd leapt the last few feet. The impact threw both men off balance and to the ground, or ice really, for they hit the frozen river hard. No cracks appeared so solid was it, but both men began to slide.

~~~

Larocque's eyes went wide when he saw Colter and the Blackfoot go down, for both were now sliding right toward him, and he on the lip of the falls. He'd been inching his way toward the pistol, but now he lunged for it, the drop be damned. He wrapped his fingers around it just as the two men hit him. The gun skittered over the edge and so too did the three men right after it.

~~~

Wolf Calf's eyes went wide at the sight, for never before had he seen a fight at the top of a frozen waterfall, and then three men go over. He started forward, but his father put an arm in front of his chest and held him there.

"No," Stone Bear said, his eyes not leaving the falls, "this is not our fight."

~~~

Small Face had seen the white man fire, Buffalo Child dodge the shot, and then the white man dodge the shot Buffalo Child had returned. After that the Wise One had gotten up and run forth, jumping into the man. Small Face already had had an arrow nocked and ready to go, but his shot had been ruined by the leap. Now Buffalo Child was over the edge, and Small Face had no way of knowing what'd happened to him, for the River Crow boy was in front of him, that ugly shield in one hand and short spear in the other.

Small Face laughed and brought up his bow. A nocked arrow was *not* a thing to waste.

~~~

Arapoosh wanted to rush to the edge of the falls and look over, for he hadn't heard a scream like he'd expect to hear a man make upon falling to his death. That's what he expected from a cowardly Blackfoot, at least, for he'd come to realize the white men he now called friends were much too strong for that.

One of those cowards stood in front of him now, a young brave not much older than himself. He had a bow with an arrow nocked, and something must have suddenly struck him as funny, for with a smile he brought the weapon up to his face and made to fire.

Arapoosh put up his shield at just the right moment, when Small Face let loose. The arrow deflected off the strong and sturdy shield bearing the image of his brother and skittered off the ice and into the snow. Arapoosh saw anger and hate in the Blackfoot's face, and he also saw the brave's chest muscle's flex as he made to reach for another arrow from his quiver. Arapoosh didn't give him the chance. With one swift motion he brought his arm up and then forward, releasing his grip on the spear as he did so. So powerful was his throw that the weapon sheared into Small Face's stomach and then clean through before exiting completely out the other side, all four feet of it, as well as a good, long strand of the Blackfoot's entrails.

Arapoosh wasn't paying much attention to that, however, for as soon as he saw his throw had connected he was rushing to the falls.

~~~

Colter dodged another kick from the Blackfoot brave above him, though this one nearly sent him flying. He was clutching a spur of ice that was sticking from the frozen waterfall, the Blackfoot Indian just above him doing the same. Below him was Larocque, a couple inches under his feet. If Colter fell, he knew the Frenchman would be falling too.

Suddenly the mountain man's attention was directed upward, though not by a kick this time, but by a voice. Arapoosh's head appeared above the lip of the falls, Colter saw, and he was speaking in his native language or perhaps the Blackfeet language, and doing so with the Blackfoot warrior above them.

"You there," Arapoosh had said, though to Buffalo Child he was just the River Crow that they'd been tracking along with the whites.

"What do you want, Crow dog," Buffalo Child said. He might have been in a tight spot, but he didn't need to grovel.

"Help me," Arapoosh said, still using the native Blackfoot tongue. He didn't want the whites to understand him, though he suspected the Frenchman probably could if his voice carried enough.

"Help *you*?" Buffalo Child scoffed. "*I'm* the one that needs help here." As if to accentuate his words, the frozen spur of ice he'd been gripping with his right hand broke and he lost balance slightly before finding another. When he turned back to face Arapoosh he did so with a slightly more shaken expression.

"I've been a captive of these two whites for weeks now," Arapoosh said, hoping the Blackfoot would believe his lie. He was also hoping the two that were somewhere behind them still stayed there. "I want to be free of them, and helping you is my way of doing that."

"Captive, huh?" Buffalo Child said, and as he did so his eyes narrowed at Arapoosh. They also darted down to look to the two whites below him, and as they did so, Arapoosh leaned out a bit to look as well. When he did so, he gave his biggest smile, then quickly let it vanish as the Blackfoot's attention came his way again.

"Alright," Buffalo Child said as he began reaching his right hand out, "but if you're lying to me–"

"Give me one hand and then the other quickly, so I can pull you up," Arapoosh said, then got to his feet, "I can't support you otherwise." He held out his hands, ready to take the Blackfoot's.

Buffalo Child narrowed his eyes again, but then reached out his hand. There was little else he could do, for he'd been hanging there looking for another handhold, and there just wasn't one. His hand met the Crow's and the boy gripped it firmly. His confidence increasing, he kicked off with his feet and threw his other hand up.

Arapoosh had been waiting for that hand to leave the frozen waterfall, and when it did, he simply let go of the Blackfoot's other hand.

"No!" Buffalo Child shouted out as he started to fall, and the sound droned on for a good eighty feet down before his body struck the jagged ice thrown up by the water's continual crashing and freezing. Arapoosh didn't see the body hit, but he did see a spray of bright red blood appear as the voice cutoff.

Colter hadn't seen it either, for his face had been buried in the ice of the falls, hoping beyond hope that the Blackfoot's body wouldn't hit him on the way down. That's what he figured was going to happen when Arapoosh had smiled at them, and he'd been right. The boy was on their side, and the mountain man was damn thankful for it.

Below him Larocque was too, but just in a different way.

"You want to get those smelly feet of yours moving?" he said to the mountain man above him. Soon the men were at the top of the falls with Arapoosh, and all three of them laughing.

"Ahem."

The three stopped their laughing quickly and looked over. There by the rock wall of the upper canyon stood two more Blackfeet, one holding Colter's rifle and the other Buffalo Child's musket.

Larocque cursed in French and Arapoosh let out a deep sigh, for there was the Blackfoot he'd talked with just a short time before, when the sun was not yet up. It was up now, peeking over the eastern mountains and just starting to bathe the area in sunlight. Colter stood impassively, his face firm, for if this was death, then so be it.

Stone Bear stood staring at the two whites and lone River Crow brave for several moments before he started forward. Then, in a most unexpected move, he twirled the rifle about so that its butt-end was sticking toward Colter. The Mountain man's eyes narrowed and he grimaced slightly, but didn't move for the gun. This was obviously a trick.

They think it's a trick, Stone Bear thought to himself, and jerked his arm slightly, showing that yes, he did indeed want the white to take the gun.

Colter reached out slowly and took the rifle. Stone Bear looked to Arapoosh and nodded at the two whites. "Speak for me," he said, and Arapoosh nodded.

Colter and Larocque looked at one another, but a moment later the Blackfoot began to speak. Arapoosh translated for them.

"You men are strong, and smart," he said, "and you have much honor." He gestured toward the falls. "One who did not was Buffalo Child, a Wise One of the Piegan tribe and leader of the Otter Band." He chuckled. "There was little wise about him, if you ask me. But then few ask me anything, for if they did, they'd hear a tale they wouldn't want to hear, one of tribe fighting tribe when they should be teaming up to fight you, the white man. That's a tale few of my people want to hear, and we've paid dearly for it."

Stone Bear paused and shook his head, looked down at the ground for a moment, to his son, and then back to the whites. "Go from this land," he said through Arapoosh, "go from it and never come back. For believe me – you men are marked, the both of you, for I'll speak of your looks and tell all of what occurred here. The stories of your courage, bravery and honor will spread, and they'll be like targets on your back for all of the tribes to see." He looked one more time to Arapoosh and nodded and said a few more words before clasping his son on the shoulder and turning about. The two began walking along the river slowly, neither looking back at them.

"What was that last?" Larocque asked after a few moments had passed and the two were well out of earshot.

"He said you have until summer," Arapoosh said. "If either of you are still in these parts come summer, the tribes will have free reign to kill you."

"So that means we're safe until then, right?" Larocque asked, looking over at Colter with a smile.

"For now," the mountain man said as he kept his

eyes on the two departing Blackfeet, "for now."

39. CLARKS FORK

It was several days later and the three were walking in the snow, the sun shining down upon them.

"There it is," the Frenchman said, pointing ahead at the body of water that had just come into view ahead of them, "your Clarks Fork."

Colter put his hand to his head and nodded. There it was, the river that would take him back up to the Yellowstone and then to the fort.

"Terrible name," the Frenchman said a moment later, "just terrible."

"If you still had the land, you could name it what you like," Colter said with a smile.

The Frenchman could only blow out his mustaches and scoff as Colter walked past. Larocque had given up his shaving routine a few days before, when they'd left the Yellowstone to head through the narrow pass between the Snowy Mountains and the Absarokas. In another week he'd look as ugly as the mountain man, the Frenchman figured.

"So I guess this is 'goodbye,' then, John Colter," Arapoosh said after a moment, and the mountain man turned back, nodded.

"That it is," he said. He walked forward and put his hands on the young boy's shoulders, though he wasn't a boy any longer, the mountain man saw; now he was the brave he'd always claimed to be. "I want to thank you for everything you've done, Arapoosh, and I hope you finally find the answers you seek."

Arapoosh nodded, and felt his chin tremble a little. He'd come to like the mountain man, despite how bad he smelled.

"I hope you'll thank me too, for all that I've done," Larocque said next as Colter straightened up.

"Oh, like losing Manuel's pistol?" Colter said. "You still owe me $5 for that, *with* interest."

The Frenchman muttered a few indecipherable curses to that, but didn't argue – he knew the Spaniard that Colter spoke of, knew how hard he could be at driving a deal.

"So it's until we meet again then," he said, and gave a bow.

"Until we meet again, Antoine," Colter said, and the two embraced for a hug.

"Be safe, John – the Blackfeet have your number."

Colter only nodded, gave another smile to both of them, and turned toward the Yellowstone. The Frenchman was right, he knew, but at that moment the mountain man didn't care – he was heading home.

CONCLUSION
BACK HOME

It was an especially nice day, with the sun shining, the snow melting, and even a few birds chirping. It was the last that appealed to Pierre Cruzatte the most, for the half-Frenchman half-Omaha Indian was reminded of his time on the Platte. That southern river appealed to him now, for it was just too damn cold this far north, too damn cold indeed.

Something on the distant horizon caught the wiry man's one eye, for he only had one, though for some reason Manuel figured he'd do fine serving watch on the wall. Pierre narrowed that eye and even put his hand up to his forehead, the better to block out the sun. Sure enough, a hundred or more yards out, was a blurry figure. Pierre reached for his rifle.

He brought the Northwest Trade gun up, all primed and panned and ready to go. Gun to face, he took aim and–"

"What the hell are you doing!" George shouted as he grabbed hold of the gun's barrel and jerked it up into the air. "That's John Colter out there!"

"*It is?*" Pierre said, rubbing at his one eye as the scout took the rifle from him, shaking his head all the while. How Manuel figured the man would do a fine job serving watch on the wall was beyond George. The scout shook his head again, then turned and put his hand to his mouth and shouted out to the men doing the everyday work of the fort below.

"Hey, hey!" he shouted, getting their attention. "It's Colter! Colter's back!"

That got the men excited and they began to scurry about. A moment later George saw Manuel come from the small room that served as his office. The Spaniard looked up at him and put his arm up to block out the sun.

"Colter's back!" George shouted to him, then began running along the ramparts and to the ladder near the fort's gate.

Out on the snow-covered flatlands between the Yellowstone and Big Horn Rivers, Colter heard the men shouting and even heard his name. A moment later the tall gates of the fort began to swing open and several men appeared. There was John Potts, the German's face bright with a smile. Hugh Hall was there, looking quite sober, the mountain man noted. Peter Weiser appeared, a hammer in his hand, for the supply boat pilot had found some other tasks to occupy his time. Colter saw them all and more. He was happiest when he saw George Drouillard appear, however, and picked up his pace after that. He was nearly at the gate when he saw Manuel Lisa appear too, and by that time he figured the whole fort had turned out for him.

"John, you've made it back to us!" George said, coming out to him and giving him a few claps on the shoulder before the two embraced in a hug.

"Almost didn't," Colter said with a smile as the other men began to gather round.

"*Oh?*" Manuel said. "The Crow guides didn't keep you safe?"

Colter scoffed. "Left me for dead was more like it!"

That got a few gasps from the men, but a few chuckles as well, for everyone could see the smile on the mountain man's face.

"What happened, John?" someone called out, then from another, "what did you see?"

"What did I see?" Colter said, putting the butt of his rifle down on the ground and leaning forward on the muzzle. "Oh, just bubbling pools of mud, steaming lakes of water, and a landscape that belongs on the moon."

"Or Hell," someone called out, and the men all laughed.

"Colter's Hell," someone else said, and the name was taken up, the men mumbling and laughing and carousing. The usual winter monotony of the fort had been broken, and they were happy with it, and having some fun, even if it was at their hero's expense.

"Colter's Hell," the mountain man muttered to himself, thinking of all he'd seen on his five months out in the wilds of the wilderness. It was a fitting name, though didn't do the area justice. He liked Yellowstone better, and intended to tell the men the first chance he got.

THE END

HISTORICAL NOTE

I'd like to thank you for reading this book. The first book in the series, *Colter's Winter*, was my 10th full-length novel and I was quite surprised it sold so well. Getting on track and quickly writing a second book just made sense.

As I said on the book's title page, I've written about Colter's actual route on my website, and I have images of the locales, both in summer and winter. You'll also find hierarchies for the various Indian tribes, something that might help you keep the characters straight. I urge you to give it a look.

So what is true and what did I make up? Well, what you've just read is a novel, though one with historical elements. John Colter did go out in the winter of 1807-8 and he did follow the course that I set. It's likely he did not see Yellowstone Falls, however, as that distinction's given to Frenchman Baptiste Ducharme, who sighted them in 1824. Captain William Clark heard about them, likely in 1806, but didn't believe the tales.

The Indians of course knew about them long before that, but we don't put much stock into what they knew or believed. That's a shame, and I decided to make Indians a much more central aspect of this book. The tribes all appeared on the Missouri in the way I present, with the Arikara coming first and then the Hidatsa and Assiniboine after that. Manuel's jaunts among them to distribute gifts are accurate, as are the men's progression up the river, and the way they did it. There was a large gathering of Assiniboine that greeted the men, and Manuel Lisa did shoo them away by firing the swivel gun.

We don't know all 50 men that were with Lisa that winter, or if it was closer to 60 men. We know some of their names, and those mentioned are accurate. There are more than enough that I don't have to make up names...yet.

Bissonette *was* shot and killed, but before Colter ever joined the party. I decided to add that bit of history for your enjoyment, and for a later book in this series.

Fort Raymond was likely reached in October and finished on November 21, though we don't know for certain when construction was completed, nor do we have even a sketch of what it looked like. The measurements given are from similar Missouri River forts of that time, taken from accounts at the Montana Historical Society's Research Center in Helena, the Montana Room of the Missoula Public Library, and the various online accounts which are worth quoting. The latter is where I got most of the information on the firearms used in this novel, and the descriptions are accurate.

Francois Antoine Larocque was a real person. He did travel where I said he did, though he went back to Montreal in 1806 and was never a captive of the Cree or any tribes. I took liberty with that for the sake of the story, and used the Cree tribe because they were a member of the Iron Confederacy and fought often with the Blackfeet. The Blackfeet are the villains in this book because they did indeed attack Colter and the band of Crow guiding him. Colter *was* injured. That's where it gets a bit fuzzy, both in this book and historically.

You see, the earliest accounts of Colter's run from the Blackfeet often got some things wrong. They had Colter being guided by Crow in the winter of 1807-8 – and that may have been true – but the incident with the attack occurred around May or June 1808. We'll have that event as it happened in our next volume.

The Crow did not abandon Colter, either in 1807 or 1808. The mountain man never met Arapoosh, either. The young brave was a real person as well, and of the Crow tribe. He was born in 1795 and would live until 1835. He was already a chief when Lewis and Clark met him in 1805, and had his shield then. It had the design I listed, that showing one of the Sky People, or perhaps his brother. Thrown into the Spring *was* taken up into the sky, or so legend has it. Mountain man James Beckwourth would see that shield when he was amongst the crow in 1830, and knew of its supernatural powers. But that's a story for another day. I have a sneaking suspicion that Arapoosh's story is far from over as well.

So where does that leave us? By my reckoning, the spring of 1808. Colter's there, and he still has several major stories to go. The next involves a run.

ABOUT THE AUTHOR

Greg Strandberg was born and raised in Helena, Montana, and graduated from the University of Montana in 2008 with a BA in History. He lived and worked in China following the collapse of the American economy. After five years he moved back to Montana where he now lives with his wife and young son. He's written more than 50 books.

www.bigskywords.com

Other Exciting Books
by
Greg Strandberg

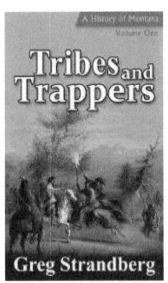

Montana history comes alive from the time of the dinosaurs all the way to 1840. Learn about Lewis and Clark and the various mountain men that came after them. Discover Montana in Tribes and Trappers!

It's been six months since the horrendous incident atop Mount Misery, the incident that broke Beldar Thunder Hammer's band of adventurers apart. Now Beldar's putting the band back together. Why? To head back up Mount Misery to end the Kingdom's Hireling system for good. A tale of epic fantasy adventure unfolds, one you won't want to miss!

1075 AD. William the Conqueror's army sits outside Norwich Castle, the siege of three months going nowhere fast. The men need ale, but there is none. One man can get it for them, Sir Peter Godfried. He sets out, and along the way he finds love, trouble, laughs, and a hideous plot to upend the kingdom in this humorous and edgy historical novella.

It's 400 BC and Seven States vie for power in the land that will become China. Marquis Wen of the State of Wei seeks to consolidate his power, and a successful siege helps with that. The other states, however, have him in their sights. Visit The Warring States today!

There's a secret underground alien base in New Mexico, one sanctioned by the federal government. But that base got away from the military in 1975. Now it's 1979 and time to take it back. Discover Dulce Base today!

Find Greg Strandberg's books on Amazon, Apple, Barnes & Noble, and other retailers

See images of the places in this book, the guns mentioned, maps showing Indian tribes, and more:

http://www.bigskywords.com/montana-blog/what-is-colters-hell

GREG STRANDBERG

Made in the USA
Coppell, TX
27 August 2022

82126602R00125